CW00847263

Peter Skillen

The Temple

© Copyright 2016
Peter Skillen
The right of Peter Skillen to be identified as author of this work has been asserted by him in accordance with the Copyright, Designs and Patents Act 1988.
All Rights Reserved
No reproduction, copy or transmission of this publication may be made without written permission. No paragraph of this publication may be reproduced, copied or transmitted, save with the written permission of the publisher, or in accordance with the provisions of the Copyright Act 1956 (as amended).
Any person who does any unauthorised act in relation to this publication may be liable to criminal prosecution and civil claims for damage.

ISBN-13:
978-1537293684

ISBN-10: 1537293680

The Temple

Also by Peter Skillen

The Twelve Step Warrior

Life is Good

The Process

Dedications

I dedicate this book to my mother and to my children: Jade, Amber, Daisy, Ava, Dexter and Ted.

Face your fears, be courageous, walk the road less travelled and live your life to the fullest.

I love you all.

Acknowledgments

Thank you to my very best friend and guide, Amanda. Without her support and encouragement this book would not exist.

Thank you to my mother for always being a light in the darkest hours.

Thank you to my sister Helen, her husband Phil and her family for providing me with my happy place; whether times are good or bad.

I was once asked if I missed my father; who passed away some years ago. I replied with a resounding, "No." Shocked, they asked me why. To which I replied, "Because he is with me everywhere I go."

Contents

The Temple

Introduction

In a distant land, there stands a snow-topped mountain with passes cut into its sides which snake precariously upward; creating what from afar, looks like a great carriageway of track. Some of these passes are wide, solid and laid with stone, making them easy to navigate, but others are mere pathways of sand and gravel; not much wider than the width of a man. These mountain pathways are a danger to all who travel them except that is, those who have navigated them through centuries past; herding their flocks back and forth on a daily basis. These shepherds of old, with ages of experience passed down from one generation to the next, use these perilous pathways to take their herds of mountain goats to graze. Twice daily, they climb the mountain using their vast knowledge to lead their flocks to the green pastures that lay on the other side, and when the sun falls behind the mountain, they herd them back to their small village, which sits in the valley at the foot of the mountain. These shepherds are an ancient people who live with nature and reside under the shadow of the mountain. Many years ago in this village, there lived a boy called Malic. This is his story; I am just the messenger who brings it to you.

Malic's home

Malic was a small boy; not much taller than the goats he herded. He lived with his mother and his father in a small wooden house; a house that was empty of material wealth, but full of love. Beautiful tapestries created by the women of his family adorned the walls and filled the house with vibrant colour. Bunches of herbs and wild flowers filled the air with scents that mingled with the fresh mountain air, and on the floor lay magnificent woven rugs; detailed with fine patterns that reflected the beauty of the mountain that stood outside.

In the centre of the round sunlit room was a large, round fire pit that looked a lot like the well that stood at the bottom of the lush green meadow outside. Above the fire hung cured meat and fresh vegetables, used to cook the daily meal in the large, black soot-burned pot that hung from an iron-forged spit. The spit, which would be used in times of celebration to roast a fattened calf, lay across the centre of the fire that for now was filled with cold burnt ash; ash that was sometimes blown across the room by the mountain breeze that blew in through the un-shuttered window, past the angel hair thin curtains, to settle on the rugs. And that was Malic's first job.

Every morning Malic would wake up on his small, rolled out mattress and start his morning chores. First, after a long morning's stretch and a yawn Malic would get dressed in his three-quarter length colourful, striped cloth trousers and pull on his white linen shirt then go out to the well at the bottom of the meadow in which his home stood.

After opening the large wooden door and closing it behind him, Malic would slip on his goatskin boots and skip to the bottom of the meadow in the morning sun; swinging his bucket as he went. Malic was a happy boy who knew nothing of the ills of the outside world; Malic's world was the meadow and the mountain.

When Malic reached the well he would lower the steel-strapped wooden bucket into the fresh, mountain spring water below and pull up the water that was needed for the day. Every morning when Malic went to the well and drew up the water, he would look out over the stone wall at the bottom of the meadow and there he would see Mila; a girl with more beauty than the spring blossom in the trees. Mila was the daughter of his father's friend who had since passed and now she lived alone with her mother; they lived in the house in the adjacent meadow. Every morning when Malic arrived at the well, Mila would be sitting out in the meadow going about her morning chores; either sitting with her mother making rugs or fetching milk from their goat. In the village where Malic lived, the women would tend to the home whilst the men would go out to work in the fields or tend their herd. Malic was never noticed by Mila, and every morning after he drew the water from the well he would make his way back to his home; satisfied that he had laid his eyes upon her.

When Malic returned to the house, his mother and father would be waiting for him and the water. His father would take the wooden bucket from him, affectionately rub him on the head then go over and pour the water into the black pot. Malic's father would then go outside and use what was left to wash with, then use the bucket to sit on whilst he milked his herd. His mother would roll up their beds whilst Malic would go to the back of the house and collect the shovel to clear the fire pit and take the old ashes outside. He would walk to the stream that ran alongside the back of his home and pile the ashes into it. The water from the stream washed away the ash and left the charcoal that would be dried out and used again. When the ashes were cleared and the herd was milked, his father would chop wood and Malic would return inside to collect the rugs. He would take them outside and using the wooden bucket as a stand, he would hang the rugs over the washing line, collect the large old tree branch that was fashioned into a beater and beat the ashes out of the rugs. The ash would fly out and hang like a feint grey cloud in the morning sun and most times, turn Malic's hair grey.

When the beating was done and the ash had settled, Malic would take the rugs back inside to where his father had lit the fire and his mother had cooked their food. Together they would sit and eat, whilst Malic would listen in to his father tell stories of the dangers of the mountain pass. Malic would listen intently as his father would tell the tale of the black wolf.

"On the mountain, high in the caves lives an old black wolf. He hides in the darkest caves waiting for unsuspecting prey. The black wolf is full of hate and some say, he was born of the darkness itself."

Malic would sit close to his mother who would pull him closer still to comfort him. "The black wolf sits and waits for the weakest of the herd and when he sees an opportunity, he will pounce. Silently, he will drag his prey into the dark recesses of his cave and sit and wait for his catch to die. The black wolf never kills his prey; he lures and injures it just enough so his victim will suffer. The black wolf is vicious and cruel and enjoys seeing the slow, painful death of his prey. The black wolf, born of the darkness, feeds on the loneliness of the weak and believes that fear is the essence of his strength. Looking at Malic, his father would warn him about the dangers of the black wolf with a poem he would never forget.

"My son, stay strong and eat your food to keep the old black wolf at bay, for he only feeds on the weak and those that stray."

Malic's mother would look at him and hold him tight, so as to reiterate the message his father was telling him, then she would kiss his forehead and go and prepare the vegetables for the meal later on that day. Malic and his father would sit at the old wooden table, his father had fashioned from an old tree and they would finish their food in silence.

When the food was eaten and the milk was drunk, Malic's father would hug and kiss his mother and hug Malic twice, kiss his forehead then leave the house to join the men of his village and take his herd over the mountain pass.

The village

The people of Malic's village were simple folk. By day, some of the men would shepherd goats and tend to their land and others would harvest vegetables and fruits to sell at the market in the town that sat at the bottom of the mountain range. The women would sew and bake breads and make beautifully woven wall hangings. They cared for each other's children and watched them as they ran free in the village square. The village was a happy place; full of tradition and love.

After Malic had cleaned the rugs and the fire was clear, he would help his mother to load the cart with vegetables and fruit from the harvest and take them to the market. Malic and his mother would join with the rest of the village children and their families and head down the mountain trail to the market. The small mule train would meander its way down the mountain path and into the valley below. Malic looked forward to this day, as Mila would also be making the same journey to help sell her families wares.

Malic couldn't quite remember the day it happened, but he remembered it was warm and particularly bright. He was a young man now and his mother was old and frail, so when his father went to the mountains, Malic made the journey to the market through the valley on his own. He knew that this journey could be his last; for one day he would have to replace his father who wasn't getting any younger, and would soon no longer be able to make the journey across the mountain pass. The rest of the villagers had been gone some time and Malic was late. He was leading his father's old mule down the mountain and as he turned the last corner into the valley, he came across Mila; the girl he had admired from afar since his childhood years.

Mila's mule had bolted and her milk urns had fallen to the floor. Malic came to a stop and joined Mila in picking them up; reloading them back onto her small cart. When the urns were back on the cart, Malic went after the mule but this mule was as stubborn as they say mules usually are. He approached the mule, but as he did it walked away and every time Malic ran a little quicker, so did the mule. Mila had taken up a seat on the edge of the cart and smiled as Malic ran aimlessly around the field trying his best to catch it. She giggled every time he got close but stumbled and fell. He took this as a personal challenge and tried his very best to capture and mount it. At one point, Malic had a hold of its reins and one leg over its back, but it rose up and he ended up hanging on for his life as it ran amok across the field. Mila stood in anticipation hoping

Malic would hang on, but the mule came to a sudden stop and he was thrown up into the air, landing in a nearby stream. For a moment Mila held her breath, but then as Malic rose from the water; his hair strewn across his face and his shirt and cloth trousers stuck to his now masculine body, she let out a sigh of relief. He looked up and watched in disbelief as the mule slowly walked over to the cart and stopped, ready for its harness to be strapped back on. Malic stood with his hands on his hips and Mila giggled with delight. It was at that moment that Malic looked up and knew that he was in love and Mila was the woman he wanted for his wife.

The market

From that day on, Malic and Mila went to the market together. One time when they visited it, they saw a small boy drawing on parchment paper and for a small payment, he would sketch a portrait. Malic asked the boy to draw Mila. Mila sat on the small rock the boy was using as a place to sit whilst he created his drawings. The boy complimented Mila and told her she was the most beautiful woman he had ever had the pleasure of drawing. This made her blush, because she didn't think of herself as beautiful at all, and this is something that Malic knew made her both beautiful on the inside as well as on the outside. Whilst Mila sat as the boy drew, Malic walked over to a market stall and bought some figs from a trader. He sat and ate the sweet fruit and watched the boy's drawing come to life. He commented on how amazing the boy's talent for drawing was, as the image of his beautiful Mila unfolded before his eyes. The boy turned to Malic and said,

"Sir, we are all given a gift from the universe. Some are born with a natural talent, whilst others find this gift later on in their lives when the universe knows they are ready to receive it." The boy never took his eyes away from his work and continued, "You see the only thing is, most of us don't even recognise our gift or forget what it is, and some are even too scared to use it for fear that that gift will not be accepted as good enough for the world. Those who do remember accept it and use it. They may not be men and women of riches, but they will have something worth far more than all the riches in the world; they will be the ones with inner peace and happiness. Malic smiled and replied,

"I wish I could find my gift." The boy turned and looked at Malic, then back at Mila,

"Maybe Sir, you already have." The boy finished his drawing of Mila and held it up for Malic to see. It was beautiful and the image he had drawn looked as if Mila herself was staring right back at him. He showed her and said,

"Look at how the boy has captured your beauty." She blushed and giggled. Malic paid the boy and took Mila by the hand as they walked through the market together. Mila noticed a stall full of fine thread and beautifully woven clothes; she smiled at Malic and walked over to it. Malic saw a stall that sold gifts made from leather and stone. There was one particular leather-bound necklace that held a deep emerald green stone, so beautiful that it reminded him of Mila's eyes, which caught his gaze. Malic spoke to the trader who owned the stall and asked him the price.

"What price can be put on love?" the trader asked him. "This is a truly beautiful stone that will be a reflection of your love to whomsoever you bestow it upon." The trader took the shoulder of Malic and told him that he had watched as Malic and Mila's love had grown over the years and how it had reminded him of the love he and his wife had shared over years of marriage. He spoke to Malic and told him that the love between them was a gift from the universe; a gift that would last forever. He told him that every morning he should talk to the universe and give thanks for the gift of Mila, then he handed Malic the leather-bound stone, "A gift from the universe; in honour of your love." Malic was hesitant but the trader insisted and told him to take the gift; if not from him, then as a gift from the universe itself. Malic accepted the necklace and thanked the trader many times, until the trader told him, "Don't thank me, thank the universe and thank it daily for your beautiful bride-to-be." Malic was taken aback a little by the trader's words. How did he know that he wanted Mila to be his wife he thought? But it was a thought that swelled his heart with love. With this, Malic left, hiding the leather-bound stone in his pocket. He re-joined Mila and together, they made their way through the hustle and bustle of the market. Malic knew that soon he would ask Mila to be his wife.

From that day on, Malic remembered to thank the universe every morning and every night for the gift of love that had been bestowed on him; of the most beautiful woman he had ever laid his eyes on. In his eyes, Mila's beauty shone like the stars in the sky; so thanking the universe seemed to make complete sense. From then on, when Malic would pass the market stall. he always remembered to thank the trader for the gift and every time the trader would say the same thing, "Remember, don't thank me, thank the universe."

Love

Malic and Mila spent most evenings walking through the valley at the foot of the mountains. They would walk for hours talking of days' past. They would reminisce about their childhood in the village, of drawing water from the well and milking the herd. Malic would talk of his mother and the beautiful tapestries she made and the grey hair that was inflicted by the ash. Mila would gaze in wonder at Malic as he spoke; she would smile and her heart would be full, for she knew this was the man she loved.

They talked about the life and the days that would come. Malic spoke of how he would one day build a house for her and about how he would have to take his own herd over the mountain pass. He spoke of how their time together would be less and the days of hard work would be longer and how he would miss their long walks in the valley at night; but having her in his life would make it worth all the hard work ahead. Malic was sure never to tell Mila of the black wolf in case it should drive her away, for fear of losing him to the mountain.

It was tradition in Malic's village that if a man wanted to marry a woman, he would ask her mother for her hand. Her mother would tell the man to build her daughter a house and if the house was to the satisfaction of the mother, she would give her blessing. Malic, wanting to ask for Mila's hand in marriage, went to his father and his mother and asked, "Tell me, how can I build a house beautiful enough to request the hand of Mila in marriage?" Malic's father took him to the outside of their house and pointed to the mountain,

"My son, a house has to be built like the mountain. Make it strong and build it with rocks from the mountain, so it will last the test of time. Build a strong foundation, for when the rain comes and the water flows into the valley, it needs to be able to repel the water and stop it from washing away the house you have built. The Mountain stays because of its strong foundation. A house built without foundation will surely fall. Secondly, you must build your walls strong to stop the autumn winds blowing them down. Malic, my son, the roof of your house should also be strong but made out of wood from the forest that surrounds the valley. If we watch the animals that live there, we see how they seek out the trees for shelter and how the trees give them life. We can see as the seasons pass, how they replenish themselves and just like this, your roof will need to be replaced. But Malic," at this, his father looked into the house at Malic's mother, "you must fill your house with love, for it is the love inside that makes that house your home." Malic knew that his father was passing on the knowledge that had been passed on to him by generations of fathers' past, a knowledge that had been borne out of sacrifice and hard work; knowledge that had been gathered by many great men and women of the village. He thanked his father and returned into the house and asked his mother,

"Mother, how will I fill my house with love?" She took his face in her hands and smiled,

"Son, treat your wife like you would your mother. Love her, protect her and provide for her; but most of all talk to her. Ask her how she feels, ask her for her thoughts and follow them. Listen to her and keep her happy." Malic smiled and said,

"I would shower her in gold and jewels if only I could." She smiled back and told him,

"Malic, the most beautiful jewels in the world have no value compared to a man of honesty and good stature. A woman who seeks only gold and jewels is not a woman of love, but a woman who receives the gift of love and respect, will fill your house with love and affection." Malic sat with his mother for a while who stroked his head and as she did, Malic closed his eyes and dreamt of the house he would build.

Jafkin

Malic's daily routine of fetching the water and clearing the fire still remained. After clearing the fire Malic would then beat the rugs and also milk the herd. Each time he carried out this daily routine, he would look across the meadow to the home of Mila, where she would be sitting weaving in the company of her mother. Except now, she would smile the most beautiful smile and this smile would fill Malic with warmth and love; giving him the most heart-warming start to the day. His father and mother were not young anymore and Malic made sure that daily, he would help them as much as he could. His father still herded the goats across the mountains to the green pastures but Malic had seen that each day, his father seemed to grow wearier and the mountain pass was taking its toll; often his father would be the last to return home.

After his chores at the house, Malic would tend to the fields and the crops he now grew. He would go to the shared stable at the bottom of the field and prepare the mule for the day's work. On this day, whilst Malic was preparing the plough and strapping his mule to it, another young man of the village, Jafkin, entered the stable. Jafkin was the son of Josiah; a rich trader who owned the market. Josiah was known as a hard-hearted man who often paid too little for the crops and wares he bought from the villagers but they could not complain because he was the only trader that came to buy them; on account of the fact that the only route into the village ran through his land. Josiah knew how lucrative trade with the village was and refused passage to all other traders that came.

This hard-heartedness had been passed down the family to Jafkin. Malic and the rest of the young men of the village had grown up with Jafkin since childhood.

Often, when they were children, Jafkin would bully and chase them or challenge them to fights he knew he could not lose. Jafkin was a big child; bigger than the rest of the boys in the village but now seemed to have shrunk in size but grown in muscle. Jafkin also had his father's ways and the villagers knew he was a man of few values. He was someone who would squeeze the last grain from a man's hand at a price far lower than his father, and compassion was not something he seemed to have. Jafkin entered the stable and looked straight at Malic, with a look that could have frozen a flowing stream. Malic ignored Jafkin and continued to prepare the mule for the fields. Jafkin asked him to water and feed his horse as he had just returned to the village after a long journey over the mountain pass. Malic said nothing and thinking more of the horse than

Jafkin's request, drew a bucket of water from the water barrel and a bucket of grain, and placed them in front of Jafkin's tall black steed. As the horse drank and ate, Jafkin surveyed Malic who had finished preparing the mule for the day's harvest. "Off to harvest the field are you?" Jafkin asked. "Be sure to only bring the best produce to sell at the market, your father's crop last year was quite meagre. This year, I'm afraid the prices paid will not be as much as last season." Malic finished strapping the mule to the harvester and walked it out of the stable. "Malic, isn't it?" Jafkin asked as Malic was nearly out of the stable door. Malic stopped,

"Yes," he replied.

"Ah, I remember you from when we were children; you were the lonely child who used to play alone or with the girls. Speaking of which, I have just seen Mila in the village. What a beautiful girl she has grown to be; someone I might quite like to know better myself." Jafkin's voice was laced with sarcasm and Malic knew that he was trying to provoke a reaction. Malic felt a surge of energy run through his body, but remained calm. This was a feeling he hadn't felt before and he didn't like it. Malic led his mule into the fields and started gathering the crops, leaving Jafkin behind laughing to himself.

Jealousy

All day as Malic worked the fields, the thought of Jafkin's words ran through his mind, and the thought of Jafkin with Mila drew emotions and feelings from deep within that he had never felt before; which disturbed him.

Later that day after Malic had toiled long and hard gathering his crops, he returned home. As he entered the house, he could smell the aroma of the spit roasted meat and spiced vegetables cooking over the fire. The aroma stirred his hunger and his appetite grew as he washed his hands and face with water from the bucket, that he had drawn that morning from the well. The water was cold and refreshing and cooled Malic's now strong body, but his mind was still full of the words Jafkin had said and his heart still burned with the emotions it drew deep from within him.

As Malic sat with his father and mother to eat, he told his mother of Jafkin's words and how the feelings had churned within him all day; filling him with a sense of sadness and anger. She looked at him with love in her eyes and then spoke in a soft voice, "Son, this is jealousy. What you are feeling is fear and insecurity and a man who lives with fear and insecurity does not live at all." Malic pondered over his mother's words. She continued. "Jealousy only hurts the person who holds it and for it to be banished, you must understand it." Malic sat and listened intently. "Jealousy is the disguise of fear and it will grow within you unless it is let go." Malic wanted to understand his mother's words and asked her to explain to him how and why jealousy had entered his heart. She explained further, "Jealousy arouses your fears. Mila is the girl you love and you fear losing her to Jafkin; fear is an emotion that can both kill your love or teach you to love stronger than ever. When we give into the fear we become weak and when we are weak, our inner anger will rise to the surface. Anger will kill your love, for an angry man only carries hate and a man who is full of hate, cannot have room for love." Malic began to understand what his mother was telling him and the love in her voice started to calm the emotions he had been feeling all day. "When we are fearful, we become insecure; we doubt ourselves and our own gifts and abilities. We doubt love; we doubt the people we love and trust is lost. When the trust is lost between two people who love one another, that love will start to wilt and die and in turn, this will cause you more pain and sorrow." Malic asked his mother,

"But how can I lose this feeling; these thoughts I have?" She took him by the hand and said,

"Let go of your fears and remember why you fell in love. Do not concentrate on that, that isn't really happening and do not put your thoughts in what could be; but instead, what is." Malic smiled at his mother and let her words fill his heart. He sat and finished his food and decided he would go and see Mila.

Moonlight walk

Malic bathed in the wooden bath that stood in the small room adjacent to the house. As he lay there in the warmth of the water, he thought about the words his mother had said to him and promised himself to rid his mind of jealous thoughts and instead, only think of the good things that he and Mila had shared. His thoughts turned to the leather-bound, emerald green stone that the market trader had given to him. Malic decided that tonight, he would give it to Mila and tell her of his plans to build her a house.

Malic dressed and left the house; he walked down to the well and sat and waited. As he waited he looked out into the valley. The air was cool and the night was drawing in. The sweet smell of the flowers in the valley reminded him of when he was a boy and how he watched Mila work and play in the fields and how he wanted to spend time with her. And now he was realising his dreams. Mila's voice broke his thoughts as she called out his name softly. Malic climbed the stone wall that stood behind the well and walked towards Mila. As he approached her, he held the leather-bound necklace tight in his hand; he would wait until the right moment to give it to her and hoped she would accept it and understand his love for her. Malic stood in front of Mila and looked deep into her clear emerald green eyes, which reflected the light of the setting sun. He raised his hand and gently cupped her face; her smooth golden skin was soft and she smelt as sweet as the wild flowers in the valley. "Are you alright, Malic?" Mila asked, with a sense of concern.

"Let's walk," Malic replied and together they walked side by side through the knee-high grass of the valley. The sun was settling behind the mountain and a full moon filling the horizon, had started to rise. As they walked towards a small gathering of rocks at the foot of the mountain, Malic gazed at Mila and clutched the leather-bound stone even tighter, anticipating what her reactions might be. His mother's words ran through his mind,

'Do not put your thoughts in what could be, but instead, what is.'

Malic smiled and thought to himself how easy it was for him to live in a future that hadn't arrived yet; instead of concentrating on the present.

When they reached the foot of the mountain they sat down. Mila sat on the soft grass and Malic sat beside her. He could feel the fear of Mila's possible rejection and his heart raced. He held the leather-bound stone tighter still but once again, his mother's words entered his head,

'Let go of your fears and remember why you fell in love.'

Malic did remember. He remembered how, when he was a young man, he had chased the mule and how Mila laughed. He remembered the days they shared going to market to trade their goods and he remembered the days they had spent together; growing up in the village. Mila looked at Malic and asked him,

"What is wrong? Something seems to be on your mind." Malic took Mila's hand and held it gently; his heart was beating hard against the inside of his chest. He placed the leather-bound stone into her hand and closed it. "What is it?" she asked. Malic took his other hand and pressed his finger gently against her lips,

"Shh," he whispered. Looking into Mila's eyes he spoke to her, "Mila, for many years since we were young, I have spent time with you, I have laughed with you, I have walked with you many times in this valley but tonight Mila, under the stars and a full moon and as the universe is my witness, I want to tell you that I love you." With this, Malic let go of her hand and Mila looked down. As her fingers uncurled, she slowly saw the leather-bound stone glistening in the light of the moon. As its reflection shone in her eyes, she felt them fill with tears and she looked up at Malic; he spoke to her, "I will build you a house and protect you as my queen. I will love you beyond all love and I will be faithful to you as long as I live and breathe." A tear fell from Mila's eye and ran down her velvet soft skin. She looked at Malic and replied,

"And I will love you as my king and fill your heart with love; as the stars fill the night sky." Malic leant forward and Mila met him half way and for the first time under the moonlit sky and the eyes of the universe, their lips met and they embraced each other tightly; both knowing that the love they shared was true.

As they ended their first kiss, Mila held up the leather-bound stone and Malic took it from her. He raised his hands and fastened it around her neck; Mila looked down at it and smiled. Together they lay back in the long grass and looked up at the bright golden moon that lit up the valley, and gazed upon the beauty of the night sky.

Jafkin's approach

The next day, the sun was high in the sky and the day was hot. Mila was sitting outside of her house dressed in a simple, white cotton dress; that against her dark skin made her beauty shine. Suddenly the sound of a horse startled her. She looked up from behind her forearm that she had raised to shade her eyes from the blazing sun and was met by the sight of a black steed raised up on its hind legs, and in the saddle was Jafkin. He was dressed in black with heavy boots but his top was a thin white cotton tunic. His long black hair moved in the breeze; much like the mane of the steed he was riding. Although Jafkin's soul was unattractive, his torso was strong and his features were undeniably handsome.

Jafkin calmed his horse and the dust settled. Mila could only see his silhouette against the bright sun but she knew it was him. Jafkin, still atop his horse, moved towards Mila who retreated into herself, "What is it you want, Jafkin?" Mila asked.

"Mila, I sense an air of disdain in your voice, surely you are pleased to see me? It's been so long." Mila composed herself and continued weaving a colourful rug. She paid no attention to Jafkin, who was now dismounting his horse. Jafkin tied his horse to a nearby gate and approached the water bucket that was next to Mila. He gestured towards the water-filled bucket, "May I?" Jafkin asked. Mila, without looking up replied,

"Drink. If someone denies even the lowliest of creatures water, they become as low as them." Jafkin laughed and bent down to the bucket and swilled his face and hair with the cool water. As he stood up, Mila noticed the water run through his hair and his strong, water-covered torso sparkled in the rays of the sun.

"Ah, there's still an old fire burning inside you I see Mila. After all these years, I thought it might have extinguished just a little." Mila turned away and without looking back up replied,

"Sometimes, a fire will re-ignite when it is touched with the same flame that started it." Jafkin moved closer,

"Maybe that fire never went out and has burned slowly since it was ignited." Again, Mila, without looking up replied,

"Some fires bring warmth and are welcomed, others bring nothing but destruction and leave the earth blackened and barren; this fire, I think, is the latter." Jafkin laughed, but this time his laugh was trying hard to hide his disdain at the insult Mila had just fired at him.

"So many years have passed Mila and as you know, some people change." She quickly replied,

"Some people, yes." Jafkin moved even closer to Mila; making her visibly uncomfortable.

"My beautiful Mila, why don't we forget the past and concentrate on the present? The end of harvest celebration is nearing, why don't you accompany me and we could get reacquainted." Mila looked up directly into Jafkin's face,

"Why would I want to spend a celebration in the company of someone, whose biggest celebration is himself?" Jafkin, clearly offended, grabbed Mila by the arm,

"There are many women in this land that would be honoured to celebrate with a man such as myself." Suddenly a voice called out from the valley,

"Mila!" it was Malic. Mila pulled her arm away and stood up as Malic entered her garden; Jafkin stood too. "Mila?" Malic asked. "Is everything alright?" Jafkin turned to Malic with a cocky smile and spoke,

"Everything is just fine; we are just old friends getting reacquainted." With that, Jafkin mounted his horse and turned to leave the garden. Malic stood next to Mila, looking at her with concern. Jafkin sat on his horse and pulled its reins high then looked at Mila and the stone that hung around her neck, and in a voice of ridicule he said, "A woman of your beauty should surely be showered in gold and diamonds instead of such cheap trinkets." Mila held her gift from Malic tight and stepped forward,

"No matter how expensive the gift, if the man who gives it has a black heart, the gift will never be precious." Jafkin, annoyed and ridiculed again, kicked into his horse, jumped over the fence and galloped away, leaving a trail of mountain dust in his wake. Malic, comforting Mila asked her what had happened. Mila held him close and told him, "Malic, my beautiful love, come, let's eat." With this, she led Malic into her house.

Mila's story

The inside of Mila's home was much like Malic's own small house; the walls were adorned with the beautiful woven fabrics she and her mother had made. In the centre of the room stood a large wooden table and on it lay cloth and thread, half-woven sheets and a carpet woven in a myriad of colours; reflecting the flowers of the valley they lived in. Mila took Malic by the hand and sat him down on a large colourful cushion that lay in the corner of the room and then walked over to the fire. Over the fire there hung a black metal pot, used for boiling water. Mila poured water from a wooden bucket that stood next to the hearth into the pot and placed some logs onto the nearly, burnt-out embers of the fire underneath it. Malic sat and watched her as she rinsed her hands in a wooden bowl, then took two wooden cups from the shelf next to the fire. Mila took some leaves from a small jar, tore them and then placed them into the cups. Next, she took a larger wooden jar and spooned fresh honey in too. The logs had now set alight and flames licked the upper outside of the fireplace, leaving a sooty mark on the iron hearth that surrounded it. Puffs of white smoke drifted through the room and the sweet aroma of the burning wood filled the air. Mila turned and looked at Malic and smiled a nervous smile, “What is it Mila?” Malic asked. As Mila turned back towards the fire, she spoke.

“Malic, I need to tell you something. I need you to listen because what I have to tell you, I don’t want it to hurt you.” Malic edged forward and thought for a moment.

“Mila, please come sit with me and tell me what troubles you.” Mila tentatively walked over to where Malic was sitting. He reached up and took her by the hand as she sat down next to him. Malic looked at Mila with concern in his eyes, “Mila, what is it that troubles you so much?” He stroked her hair and gently cradled her face. Mila carefully took hold of Malic's hand and pressed it firmly onto her cheek; rubbing it into his firm but gentle hands. She sighed then raised her other hand and clasped his hand inside her own, resting them on her lap.

“Malic, many years ago before we used to walk in the valley together, Jafkin and I had become close. Malic felt an uneasiness rising in his stomach but he listened as Mila spoke. “Jafkin would bring the thread and the cloth to my house after my father and mother had been to market. He was a happy soul who would always bring me small trinkets and the best fruit from the market traders.” Mila gently caressed Malic’s hand as she continued, “My father would always tease me and say that maybe Jafkin, the son of the rich market owner would eventually be my love." Malic felt his stomach turn over inside like a wave rising through the sea. He knew it was once again, jealousy rising and this made him feel uncomfortable. Jealousy was a new emotion for Malic as his life had been so simple until now, and everything he ever had, he had shared. He fought to calm the feelings that rose inside him and kept his attention on Mila's words; wanting to listen, but not wanting to hear of his lifelong love in the arms of another man. Mila continued, "On the evening of the festival of the harvest and at the market square, my father was talking to Josiah, Jafkin's father and although we come from very different families; me, the daughter of a goat herder and a weaver and Jafkin, the son of a rich market owner, it was decided that we would walk together alone and talk about a future together." Malic's heart sank; his mind raced as he imagined Mila not being a part of his world anymore now Jafkin had returned to the village. Mila felt Malic's hands tremble and as she did, she held them tighter and continued, "That night Malic, we walked in the fields on the outskirts of the village. Until this time Jafkin had always made me smile and I had looked forward to the day he would deliver the thread and cloth to my home. As we walked, we came to the well and Jafkin took my hand." Malic's heart was growing heavier the more

Mila explained. The feelings in his stomach had turned to crashing waves and his breathing had quickened with anticipation of Mila's next words. "He moved closer and stood in front of me and walked forward until my back was against the wall of the well. I couldn't move and I asked him to retreat, but instead he lowered his head and tried to kiss me. I shunned him and pushed him away; telling him to show me more respect, but instead he pushed me back and kept trying to kiss my face. It was at this point my mother shouted out and Jafkin let go of me." Malic's jealousy had turned to anger that was growing inside of him; it was like a storm had risen deep within and he could feel his blood surging through his veins. He tried to talk but Mila pushed her finger to his lips. Mila looked up at Malic and he looked into her emerald green eyes that were now half-full with tears, and she spoke again, "My mother took me home and told me never to speak of what had happened to my father, as he would confront Jafkin and in turn, his father, a very powerful man, may not supply us with the thread and cloth we needed to survive." Mila let go of Malic with one of her hands and wiped a tear that had fallen down her beautiful, soft olive skin. Malic was about to comfort Mila but she took hold of his hand once again, "My mother has never told me what she told my father about what happened that night, but from then on she insisted that he would take the mule to market and bring the cloth home himself." Malic's eyes too, filled with tears, tears of anger coupled with sadness at the sight of his beautiful Mila in a moment of brokenness; something he had never witnessed before. He sat for a moment, his hands still clasped inside hers. Suddenly the sound of steam splashing onto the embers of the fire took Mila's attention away from the moment. She stood, wiped the tears from her face and walked over to the boiling black pot of water. Wrapping a cloth around the handle, she took it from the hook that held it over the flames and poured it into the cups over the leaves and honey. She then placed the pot back on the hook, took two sprigs of mint from bunches of herbs that hung above the fire and added them to the cups. She walked back over to Malic, who took both cups from her hands and placed them next to the cushion they were sat upon. Again he took her by the hand as she sat down next to him, drew her closer and cradled her in his arms. Mila laid her head in the nape of his neck and as they sat together, Malic contemplated what Mila had told him.

A father's advice

Later that night when Malic arrived home, his father was sitting by the stream with his feet in the cool, fresh running water. Once a week, his father sat in the same spot and looked upon the mountain whilst drinking a wine reserved for the shepherds. Malic approached his father who gestured him to sit. He slipped off his boots and sat down next to him. Malic's father, his gaze still focused on the mountain, asked him what was wrong. Malic smiled to himself and wondered how he had sensed his upset; something he had always been able to do since he was a small boy. Malic looked into the water and asked his father,
"Father, what would you do if you knew that in the past, someone had hurt my mother?" His father sat in silence for a moment, took a drink of the wine then replied,

"My son, what is done is done; you cannot change the past with either war or peace. The past is the past and it will never be the present or the future again." Malic listened as his father continued, "When you live to a certain age my son, you realise that trying to change the past is the game of a fool; you can only ever live in the present. Living in the past and trying to change the future will not change the course of what is gone, or of what is to come."

"But wouldn't you want revenge?" Malic asked. His father poured some more wine from a carafe into his wooden cup, drank from it and replied,

"What is revenge, but another evil deed that relights the fire of the first?" Malic sat and listened as his father continued, "Malic, revenge and hate will not undo what is done; only love can do that." Malic quickly replied,

"But it's so hard not to have thoughts of revenge."

"Thoughts are not actions," replied his father, "but remember, the universe also sees your thoughts." His father asked him to go into the house and fetch another cup, which he did. On his return, Malic's father filled both cups and offered one to him. Malic was hesitant as he had never drunk the wine before, but his father gestured him to drink. Malic raised the cup and drank the wine. At first it took his breath away and filled his throat with what felt like fire, then as quickly as the fire in his throat was ignited, it was extinguished and replaced with a warm feeling throughout his chest which seemed to permeate right through his body; warming him through. His father looked at him and smiled, "Son," he said, "sometimes it is better to sit back and watch our enemies destroy themselves." Then he filled Malic's cup and they both sat at the foot of the mountain for the rest of the night; drinking the wine, with their feet dangling in the cool water of the stream.

Mother

The next day Malic awoke, his head was sore and his mouth was dry. The sun shone in through the window, blurring his vision. He rubbed his eyes and face, and stroked his hands through his hair. When he fully opened his eyes, he saw his father standing at the end of the bed. Malic instantly knew something was wrong,

"Father, what is it?" Malic asked. His father's eyes filled with tears as he moved over and sat on Malic's bed.

"Son, she has gone." Malic sat up confused,

"Who has gone Father?" A tear fell from his father's eyes as he took hold of Malic's hand and pressed it between his own.

"Last night your mother fell asleep in my arms, but today she didn't wake." Malic's heart sank and for a moment he was frozen. The tears flooded his eyes and his soul seemed to run from his body. Instantly he was plunged into a vacuum of silence; his veins ran with deep sadness. As he looked into his father's eyes, he saw the remnants of a broken-hearted man looking back. Malic reached out and held his father tight, and together they wept.

After a short while, Malic left his father's embrace and stood; leaving him sitting on the bed with his head in his hands. Malic walked hesitantly towards the bedroom door. He didn't want to leave the company of his father but he knew that this was something he could not run away from. Malic left the bedroom and walked into the centre room of the house. There across the room lay his mother. Malic walked towards her; his eyes once again filled with tears and his heart was heavy. Malic's mother lay on her bed dressed in her white night clothes; the glow of her skin was golden and radiated across the room. To Malic she didn't look lifeless; with the sun glowing on her face, she looked like an angel. There was a smile on her face and a look of serenity; he knew she was at peace. Malic approached the bed and knelt down beside his mother; he stroked her forehead and her hair and looked upon her face. The feeling of sadness crept through his veins and into his heart that hung heavy in his chest. A tear rolled down his face and his breath stuttered as he leant over to kiss her cheek. He knew this would be the last kiss he would ever lay on his mother's face and he cried; his heart was broken. Malic embraced his mother and held her close. He wanted her to wake up and comfort him, like she would when he was a child in her arms. He remembered how his beautiful mother had guided him through his life. How, when his father was away on the mountain, she would sit by his bed and read to him by candlelight. He remembered how she would smile at him as he played in the fields and how he would sit and watch her weave her beautiful rugs. He remembered how she would clean and prepare the house for his father's return and how on that return, she would look at his father with a love, purer than the water in the mountain stream. As Malic lay embracing his mother, he felt a hand upon his shoulder. He turned and looked up into the eyes of the only other woman he had ever loved; Mila. She knelt down next to Malic as he laid his mother onto the bed and left his mother's arms for the final time. He turned to Mila and she embraced him. Malic cried into the nape of Mila's neck and she comforted him; she stroked his hair and held him tight as Malic sobbed. She knew he had lost the light of his life.

Malic's father entered the room and walked over to Mila and Malic. He looked upon his wife and took a deep breath. Malic looked up as his father who spoke to his wife, "My love, you have brought me the happiest days of my life and you have given me the greatest gifts. Sleep well and dream beautifully my perfect love." With this, he lifted the throw that covered her body, kissed her forehead then covered her face. Malic and Mila rose and stood either side of Malic's father and put their arms around him. Together they turned and walked out of the house. They stood outside in the sunshine and a crisp, fresh breeze blew through the valley. Malic's father smiled as he felt the wind on his face, “She lives on the wind and has returned to the mountain.” He looked up to the blue sky and spoke gently, “Goodbye my love.”

The spirit of the mountain

The next day, Malic's house was full of the women of the village. They mourned the death of Malic's mother and prepared her body. They dressed her in her finest clothes, as the men of the village built a pyre. The night fell and the villagers gathered around the pyre. The night sky was full of stars, and the moon lit up the valley with a beautiful blue light. His father came out of the house and behind him the men of the village carried his mother on a wooden stretcher; laden with beautiful coloured weaves and wild flowers from the valley. The women of the village sang sweetly as his mother was raised onto the funeral pyre. Against the shadow of the mountain and under the blue moonlit sky, Malic's father approached the pyre with a flaming torch and lit it. It ignited and smoke surrounded his wife as Malic and Mila stood and looked on. Mila squeezed his hand tightly and rested her head against his shoulder; comforting him. Malic stood looking into the flames that started to rise and then took one last look at his mother's beautiful face before the smoke rose and took his mother out of view. The women of the village finished singing and joined the men who, one by one, passed by Malic's father; acknowledging him with a bow of their head as they did. He stood silent, staring into the flames of the fire that would return the empty vessel that once held his wife's soul, to the mountain.

When the villagers had left, Malic and Mila walked over to his father who stood motionless, and together they bowed their heads. His father's face remained expressionless, apart from a single tear that fell down his weathered face. Together, Malic and Mila walked towards the house; but just before entering, Malic turned. He saw the silhouette of his father against the flames of the fire as they licked the sky, and from the distance, a lonely howl of a wolf filled the air. Mila put her arm around Malic and they entered the house; leaving his father alone to say farewell to his wife.

Mourning

A month had passed since Malic's mother's funeral, and Malic hadn't worked the fields since. He hadn't seen Mila and she had let him grieve, in a way only a man would grieve the loss of his mother; alone and in silence. Malic was sitting outside his house by the stream looking into the water; it was then his father joined him. He sat down next to him and for a moment he stayed silent, then he spoke, "Malic," he said, "I know you are missing your mother and your heart is as heavy as mine, but we have to continue. We cannot hide away and let life pass us by." Malic turned to his father,

"But I miss her so much." Malic's father replied,

"Malic, life is like the water in the stream. We know not its true source and we know not where it flows and nor do we search for these answers. But what we do have is faith that every morning we wake, the stream will be flowing right here enabling us to draw from it. Malic, the stream is like life; it is long and ever-flowing, but as we sit here, the water will only pass us by but once." Malic turned to his father and gazed upon his weathered face; hanging on to every word he spoke. Malic's father continued, "Once the water has passed us by it has gone forever; like moments in life, it will never return. We either draw from it or we let it pass us by." Malic listened intently as his father continued, "If we did not draw our daily water from the stream, we would not survive for long and it is the same with life; we must draw from it and what it presents us with, before it passes by." Malic turned and reached out his arms and held his father tight. His father spoke quietly to him, "Do not let life pass you buy; go to Mila and build her a house." Malic's heart leapt and his mind seemed to awaken. He had been so wrapped up in himself with grief, he had forgotten about the woman he loved and he hoped she had not forgotten him. Malic drew back from his father's arms and looked him in the eyes,

"Thank you Father." With this, he released his embrace, stood up and made his way to Mila's home. His father smiled to himself as he too got up and made his way to the field, to tend to his herd.

Malic approached by way of the field and past the well he stood at so many times as a young boy admiring Mila as he drew up the water. Mila was sitting in her garden weaving. He stood for a moment and remembered how through his young life, he had fallen in love with the girl who sat and weaved and now at this moment, it was time to make her his wife. He crossed the meadow to Mila and as he did, she looked up and saw him as he approached her. Her heart swelled and her spirit lifted as she rose to her feet and walked as quickly as she could towards him; Malic too walked faster. As they met in the middle of the meadow, they embraced and held each other tight. Malic pulled back and looked at Mila, "I am so sorry I have shut you out." Mila put her forefinger to Malic's lips and quietened him,

"My love, you needed time to come to terms with your loss and if we are to be married, we must both understand that sometimes it is better to sit back and allow each other time to be with ourselves. Although you were not in my sight, it doesn't mean you were not in my heart." Mila's words filtered through to Malic's heart and filled his soul with joy.

"Mila, my beautiful Mila, I have always loved you and always will, and it is today I will ask your mother if I may build you a house." Mila, knowing what this meant, looked at Malic and spoke,

"My beautiful Malic, nothing would please me more than to live in a house you have built." Malic was filled with joy at Mila's response and pulled her into his arms and in that moment, in the middle of the meadow that once separated them as children, their love for each other was made as one.

Malic returned home to his father and told him the news that Mila had accepted his offer to build her a house. His father smiled and walked over to the end of the room, beside where he sat in his chair. He pulled back a curtain that covered a small wooden table and took out a carafe of wine. "Tonight, we will celebrate," said his father, and together they drank wine and sang the traditional songs of the mountain people, long into the night.

The next morning, Malic awoke feeling like his mule had dragged him through the fields and back again. His head pounded and the feeling of warm calmness the wine had given him the night before, had now changed to one of dizziness, and the feeling of wanting to empty the contents of his stomach onto the floor. Malic stood up and as he did, the room span and his head cracked. He felt himself falter so reached out to the wall to steady himself. He staggered over to the water bucket, took it outside to the stream and filled it with the cold fresh mountain water. He lifted it high over his head and poured the water over himself. Its coldness took his breath away; shocking him, but bringing his body back to life. He went back into the house and got dressed. Today he would find a place to build a house for his bride-to-be.

Malic tried eating some food before he left the house, but the feeling in his stomach had not quite gone and the thought of eating made him feel sick. Instead, he took a carafe of water and left.

Malic was walking through the valley admiring the beauty of the day whilst he thought about how much Mila loved those walks too; how the wild flowers, the animals and the birds that lived there, excited her. His heart was warm and he knew that the valley was the place he would build his house. Up ahead on top of a mountain track, was a clearing in the land; next to a small wood where a stream ran through. Malic climbed the short path and inspected the area. There would be plenty of logs for a fire from the woods and the small stream that ran alongside the clearing would provide water for the house. The platform was halfway up a slope, so if the valley should flood, they would be safe and in the winter the mountain would shield the house from the snow that would fall. Malic walked to the edge of the platform. The view from it allowed him to see right along the centre of the valley; he knew that Mila would sit outside weaving and this view would please her. Malic decided that this would be the place he would build his house.

After a while, Malic returned home and spoke to his father. He told him of the clearing he had found and that he would start to build the house as soon as he could save the money for the few things he would need to buy; supplies such as nails, a spit for the fire and cooking pots for the stove. The rest, Malic would make from the stone that filled the valley, and the woods close by. His father asked him to make some tea and left the room. Malic poured water from the bucket into the black pot and placed another log on the fire below it. He prepared two cups and waited for his father to return. After a few moments the water boiled and Malic poured water into the cups. Just as he finished, his father returned carrying a small wooden box. He sat at the table and gestured to Malic to join him. Malic took the cups and sat opposite his father at the table. His father took his tea and as he drank, he pushed the box forward towards Malic then smiled. Malic looked down at the box and then back at his father, "For me?" he asked in a surprised voice. His father nodded. Malic undid the brass clasp on the dark wooden box and lifted the hinged lid. He looked down and his eyes lit up: his father smiled knowingly to himself. Malic was speechless. His father smiled then spoke softly,

"For you. For your house."

"But how? Where did it come from?" Malic replied. His father placed his cup on the table and took Malic's hands into his own. His hands where rough and weathered and his skin had been made dark and thick like leather. The years of working in all weathers herding his goats back and forth over the mountain had toughened his hands and made strong his grip.

"My boy, I have always told you to live in the moment and live for today, for we cannot control what is gone, or what is yet to come. But my boy, we can prepare for it just in case." Malic's father smiled and stood up and lifted his cup, drank his last drop of tea and took his crook from the corner of the room, tilted his hat and smiled. Malic looked up at his father and admired him; in his mind, he was hoping that one day, he might be as wise and as loving as his father was. His father was leaving the house and as he got to the door, he turned and looked at Malic, "What are you waiting for? The house will not build itself and today is market day." Malic suddenly remembered that today was indeed, market day; the fog of the previous night's drinking had confused his mind. His father turned and left the house to tend to his herd. Malic stood up and reached inside the box, he poured out some coins that his father had saved over the years into his hands and placed them into a small leather pouch, pulled the strings tight to seal it and left the house.

Malic made his way to the market on his cart, pulled by his old mule. He would go and see his friend the trader, who had given him Mila's beautiful necklace. When he reached the edge of the market, he tethered up the mule and cart. Walking through the hustle and bustle of the square, excitement filled his chest and the aroma of cooked meats and fine spices that hung in the air, reminded him of his mother's cooking. Malic walked through the myriad of stalls; getting lost amongst the brightly coloured silk scarfs and tripping over the loose livestock than ran around.

Chickens flew into Malic's face. The market seemed vibrant today and busier than ever before. Malic, wafting the flying feathers of the startled chickens out of his face, turned around and bumped straight into Jafkin who spun around and stared at Malic. Not realising it was Malic at first; Jafkin pushed him hard in the chest, calling him, 'Boy' and telling him to 'mind his step'. It was then, he realised who it was.

"Ah Malic, forgive me, I mistook you for one of these local peasants. When father comes to market to celebrate his day of birth, so many of these scrounging little peasants come out, hoping to get a piece of his wealth. Funny really, how when my father gives away a few coins, people seem to crawl out of their caves." Malic knew that Jafkin was meaning him when he said this, but he was so excited about the house that he was going to build that he didn't let it affect him at all. "So Malic, what brings you into market today? You're not riding that magical steed of yours I see." Jafkin was sarcastically referring to Malic's old mule and he knew that Jafkin was spoiling for an argument, so avoided feeding his negative words.

"Oh, I'm just gathering a few tools and nails, a few pots and pans." Malic stepped around Jafkin and started to walk away. Jafkin retorted sarcastically, "What are you doing, building a new stable for your mule?" Malic smiled, knowing the answer he was about to give would silence him,

"No, a house." And with that, he left. Malic's words had pierced a hole through Jafkin's sarcastic armour and shot an arrow of jealousy straight into his heart. He knew that Malic and Mila were to be married and that, he didn't like at all.

Malic hurried through the market and came to the trader's stall. The trader greeted Malic with open arms and smiled, "My boy, welcome. It's been a long time. Sit with me and tell me how you have been." The trader walked Malic to the back of his stall that was covered by a large tent and sat him down. A young man brought them tea. The trader turned to Malic and handed him a cup, and as he did, he sensed something was on Malic's mind, "Tell me Malic, what troubles you?" Malic told the trader of his mother's passing and how for a month, he had ceased to work and had been stuck in his home, unable to get out of the house; because of the deep sadness he had felt. The trader looked at Malic with concern in his eyes, "My boy, when we lose someone we love it will hurt; it is a natural reaction. Why wouldn't we feel great sadness at the loss of someone we love?" he explained. Malic knew the trader was a good man and his words comforted him. "And the girl?" the trader asked. Malic explained to the trader how he had given Mila the leather-bound stone and that he had told her he had wanted to build her a house. The trader smiled, "Always before something beautiful happens, we have to struggle; it is the universe testing us and preparing us for the next step. The universe is making sure you are ready for the journey ahead." Although Malic felt confused, he saw sense in the words of the trader. He knew that the trader was a wise man and he had nothing but goodwill for him. Malic continued,

"My father has worked all his life in the mountains and my mother sold her wares at this market to feed and take care of our family, but what I didn't know was that all the time, they were saving this for me." Malic showed the trader his pouch of coins.

"Ah, a wise man does not spend his coin in a single day; he lives for the moment but prepares for the future that may come." Malic now understood what his father had told him earlier that day, when he had given him the box. "So what is it you need?" the trader asked. Malic told the trader that he needed tools, nails and metalwork for his stove and his house. "You will need to go and see the blacksmith at the edge of the market. He will provide you with all of these things; go there now and tell him I sent you." He stood up and thanked the trader, who wrapped his arms around Malic and embraced him. "My friend, when you have the intention, you can create anything your heart desires and the universe will conspire to help you along the way; but remember, life never comes without its tests." With this, Malic left the trader's stall and as he was walking away into the chaos of the market square, he turned to the trader and called to him,

"But what is your name?" The trader smiled,

"Tell him Tobias has sent you." Malic smiled and disappeared into the market.

As Malic was making his way through the packed market square, he saw a commotion ahead. Josiah, Jafkin's father, had entered the market. He was riding a fantastically decorated carriage and was surrounded by men on horseback. Jafkin's father was the richest trader in all of the known country and although he was a shrewd and hard-faced man, on his birthday every year, he would come into town and in a display of his wealth, would throw coins into the air for the people of the surrounding villages to gather. Although this was a generous gift, he also knew that the only place they could spend it, would be in the market he owned. Malic continued on as Josiah threw coins into the crowded market and the people of the villages gathered them up. Malic had no desire to gather the coins as he had all he wanted from his father's gift.

Malic approached the forge and entered. Inside the ironmonger was standing hammering steel on the large anvil that stood in the centre of the barn.

The air was hot and filled with sparks that resembled the colours of the setting sun. The sound of the hammer hitting steel, filled the room and echoed through Malic's ears; almost deafening him. In the corner next to the large furnace, a small blackened-faced boy worked the bellows with his foot, feeding the flames with the air that made them grow higher and hotter with every downward press. The smoke-filled room, the sight, the sounds and the smell of the forge reminded him of what he imagined when his mother told him the story of how the mountain was forged by the great spirit of the universe. Malic stood for a second; in awe of what he saw when suddenly, he was taken out of his trance and prodded by the ironmonger. "Can I help?" he asked. Malic shook his head as he brought himself back to the present moment,

"Yes, I think so." The ironmonger lifted his hat high onto his forehead,

"Well I haven't got all day, there's work to be done and it won't do itself." Malic apologised,

"I'm building a house and I need tools, a stove, some cooking pots and nails." Malic poured out the coins into his hand and offered them up to the ironmonger. The ironmonger looked down at the coins then called out to the boy on the bellows, who came running over and took them from Malic's hands.

"Fourteen days," the ironmonger said, "and I will deliver the stove. The tools and the nails are over there; take one bag, a hammer and a saw." Malic looked over to the corner where a stack of large sacks of nails was piled; alongside a selection of tools.

"Thank you, Malic said, "I will let Tobias know that you have helped me, more than enough." The ironmonger again shouted out,

"Boy, bring me those coins." The boy returned and held up the coins. The ironmonger reached out and picked half of the coins from the boy's hands and handed them to Malic. "Any friend of Tobias is welcome here," said the ironmonger. Then he turned, picked up his hammer and returned to the anvil. The boy smiled at Malic then ran back to the bellows and started pushing them down faster than before. The ironmonger's hammer fell and once again, the barn was full of noise, sparks and all the colours of the sun.

Malic made his way back to his cart and loaded it with the tools and nails, climbed on and slowly made his way home. On the way back, Malic was to pass by Mila's house; so as he went through the valley, he stopped and picked wild flowers to take to her. He thought about Mila constantly and about how they would be happy in the house he would build. He thought about how together, their love for each other would turn that house into a home. How he would eventually take over from his father and herd his flock over the mountains to the pastures on the other side. He dreamed of the children that they would raise; a girl, and a boy to carry on his name. He thought about his father's gift and how he too would put aside coins for the future of his sons and daughters. Malic was an only child and had often wondered what it would be like to have had a sister or a brother, and he promised himself in that moment, that he would ask Mila for two children or more; for sometimes, the nights and days were lonely and a sister or brother, would have brought light to the darkest times.

Malic reached Mila's house and as he approached, he heard shouting. He listened intently; it was Jafkin's voice he heard and Mila was screaming. He threw down the flowers he had gathered, jumped down from the cart and ran towards Mila's house. As he got closer, he heard the slap of skin on skin. His heart raced and a surging fire erupted in his stomach. He ran towards the door and without stopping, kicked it open. There on the floor was his beloved Mila and above her was Jafkin. His hand was raised and he was about to strike Mila across the face. Malic ran forward and struck him in the side of the head. Jafkin fell to his knees. Mila called out Malic's name but Malic, so enraged, took no notice of her cries and grabbed Jafkin by his long black hair and dragged him out of the door. He struggled and screamed at Malic to let go. He did so and started striking him again and again; hitting him all over his body. Jafkin could do nothing but roll around on the floor. Mila's frail mother came out of the back garden where she had been weaving and the children and the people of the village started to gather round. Malic took hold of Jafkin by the back of his collar and dragged him across the ground towards the well. Jafkin struggled, but Malic's anger had given him strength he never knew he had. He pulled Jafkin to the edge of the well and grabbed the back of his trousers. He started to lift him; his only thought was to throw him into the deep darkness of the well where he belonged. Suddenly, a strong hand grabbed Malic and Mila's voice rang out, “Malic no! Please stop!”

The strong hand covered his own hand and he recognised it immediately; it was his fathers. Malic had been taken over by the red veil of anger. It had blocked out all of his senses, but in a single second, the sound of Mila's voice and the sight of his father's hand pulled him back from under the red veil. Malic stopped and let go of Jafkin. He turned to his father, who guided Malic behind him and into the arms of Mila. Time seemed to have slowed down whilst his rage had taken over, but now it seemed to speed up and it felt like everything had happened in a split second. Malic comforted Mila and watched as his father lifted Jafkin back to his feet. His face was bruised and his nose bled. He looked at Malic and shouted,

"You will pay for this," and with that, he walked back to his horse that was tethered to Mila's fence, and rode off at speed towards the market. Malic's father came over to him and took him from Mila's arms. He led him towards home and Mila and her mother followed.

When they reached the house, Malic's father sat him down and Mila joined them. He filled the pot with water and stoked the fire. Malic turned to Mila, "Mila, what happened?" She wiped the tears from her eyes,

"Malic, I came to see you this morning but your father told me you had gone to the market, so I came back home. When I arrived, Jafkin was at my house waiting for me." In the background, Malic's father prepared cups for tea and listened on. "Jafkin said he had seen you at the market and that you had tried to ridicule him; telling him that you were better than him and that you were going to build me a house." Malic's anger once again started to manifest itself deep within him. "When I told him it was true, he became angry and tried to tell me that you weren't worthy of my hand and told me that he was the one I should marry." Malic was desperately holding in his anger so as not to frighten Mila any more than Jafkin already had. His father took the water from the stove and poured it into the cups. Mila continued, "When I told him, you were the only person I had ever truly loved, he became angry and hit out at me and that is when you arrived." Mila's words of love for Malic instantly extinguished the flames of anger within him, and it was replaced by love. Malic reached out and wrapped his arms around Mila. His father came over to the table and placed two cups onto it, then took a third over to Mila's mother. She thanked him with a smile. He stood in front of the fire and sipped from his cup, before speaking,

"That boy is no good and never has been. His father is a shrewd businessman and commands a lot of respect, but even he has shown respect for people and love for his wife. I will go and see him tomorrow and explain what has happened; father-to-father. He gestured with his cup towards Mila and Malic, "Drink, it will calm your feelings." Malic and Mila sat with Mila's mother and drank their tea.

Josiah's story

The next day, Malic arose early to find that his father had already left the house. The summer was drawing to a close and the grey clouds had started to hang low over the top of the mountain. Malic washed in the flowing stream and could sense that the water had become cooler. The season for storms was close and he knew that if he were to build his house, it would have to be soon; before the storm season arrived. Malic went inside and got dressed. He was sure to wear an extra top, as the nights were now colder. It was a long-sleeved, leaf green tunic that his mother had made him and as he pulled it over his head, he could smell the scent of her. He breathed deeply and tried to disperse the sadness that welled up inside him. Malic let out a deep sigh as his thoughts turned to the previous day, and the rage that had reared its ugly head. Malic had never before experienced such a rage, and it had scared him. The surge of anger he had felt whilst fighting with Jafkin, was intoxicating; but he feared it. He swore that he would never again let his anger control his actions. Just then, his father returned.

"Malic, come and sit with me." He joined his father at the table. "Malic, I have been to see Mila's mother and she told me what has happened. Mila also told me what happened in the past, between her and Jafkin." Malic sat and listened. "I have also been to see Josiah, Jafkin's father." Malic feared what he would say next, but continued to listen intently. "I have known Jafkin's father since we were boys. When we were young, we worked the fields for our fathers together. Josiah and I worked hard together, but whilst I concentrated on working for my father, Josiah had a knack for making money and although his morals were questionable, Josiah seemed to attract money." Malic was starting to wonder why his father was telling him all this, but listened to what he had to say. He continued, "Josiah was a tough trader and would buy anything he could sell for ten times more; until eventually he didn't have to work the fields at all. But he was a good young man and shared his wealth." Malic's father asked him to pass him some of the wine they had drunk beside the stream. Malic got up and took out a carafe from behind the curtain. It was unusual for his father to drink so early, but since his mother had passed away, he had drunk more. He never got drunk, but he always seemed to keep it close to hand; Malic thought the wine must help comfort him. He sat back down as his father poured himself a small cup of the wine and gestured Malic to return it to behind the curtain. "Malic, Josiah was once in love as you are. He married and his wife gave birth to Jafkin, but in that birth, Josiah lost the woman he loved and Jafkin lost his mother. This changed Josiah; he concentrated more and more on his business and money. It made him a hard man, but the love of his young wife still lives within him. The reason he throws his money away each year on his birthday, is because it was the same day his wife was taken away and it stands as a testament to his departed love's effect on him." Malic's father took a drink of spirit and continued, "Malic, I am telling you this because I want you to understand what love can do to a man. Sometimes, it can make you a better man and sometimes, if the love is not true, it can turn a man into a monster." Malic knew his father was referring to Jafkin. "Malic, I have spoken to Josiah and told him of your love for Mila and also of Jafkin's actions. Josiah has summoned Jafkin to his house and will tell him that he is never to approach you or Mila again, and I am now asking you to do the same. In honour of our friendship as young men, this is what has been decided. Do you agree?" Malic heaved a sigh of relief and agreed.

"Thank you Father," his father smiled,

"We will never speak of this again." Malic agreed. "Now go, you have a house to build." Malic squeezed his father's hands then stood up and left the house. As he went out of the door into the meadow, he saw Mila sitting with her mother; she smiled at him and her mother looked up and smiled too. Malic knew that today would be the start of a new life for him and Mila.

Malic builds a house

Malic gathered his tools and his nails, along with some food for the day and his father's axe. He strapped them to his cart that his old mule then led through the meadow, down into the valley. After walking for a while, he reached the place where he had chosen to build his house. Malic led the mule up the small mountain trail, and came to rest on the level ground next to the woods. He unstrapped his tools and nails and let his mule roam free. Malic went straight to work and measured out an area for the base of his house. It wouldn't be a big house, but it would have all he needed for his life with Mila and room to expand later, when the children he so wished for, would be born. Malic marked out the house with a central room and a small bedroom at one side. He planned the stove at the back of the house, so when the meals where cooked, it would be easy to draw water from the stream that ran behind where the house would be. He also thought this would be the perfect place to put a room for them to bathe, as it would be easy to transport the warm water from the stove. Malic marked out a space for a deck at the front of the house, where Mila could sit and weave and look out onto the beautiful valley below. He stood back and worked out how high he would build the house so he knew how much wood he would need for its construction. Malic then took his axe and went into the woods. He found five trees of similar height and felled them; these would be the four corners and the central column for the house. He dragged them, one by one; to the clearing he had marked out and started to sink them into the ground. Malic toiled all day and night; he knew that to succeed in building his house, it would take time and effort and long days of hard work. But it was something he was prepared to do in order to create a home for him and Mila.

After a long day working, Malic returned home to find Mila there. She had cooked him a meal; a tureen of spiced vegetables, meat and mixed herbs. The fragrant smell of spice and mountain herbs filled his nostrils, and his stomach rumbled with anticipation; causing them both to laugh. Malic was so pleased and felt so happy that soon, this was how life would be for good.

Malic continued to work on the house for long days; well into the night, and in only four weeks, the house had taken shape. The stove had been delivered and set in and he had built a base for his and Mila's bed. Today was the day he would take Mila to the house, and show her the home he had built for them. Malic made his way to Mila's house; she too knew that today was the day that he would show her the house, and was just as excited as he. Malic went to the stable and fastened his mule to the cart. Over the weeks in-between building the house, Malic and his father had been making wooden furniture for it; a table and chairs for the kitchen, a wooden bath for the room next to the stream and a chair big enough for two, made from the softest reeds he could find. He had gathered the pots and pans he had ordered from the ironmonger and the cart was full. Malic unhitched the mule and led it out of the stable. His chest was full of anticipation, but his heart was full of love. The sky was blue and the sun shone down into the valley, but high on the mountain, snow had fallen and Malic knew that before long, the valley would be overcast and the storms that came every year would soon arrive. A slight breeze of cold air pierced the warmth of the sun and sent a shiver down Malic's spine. He shuddered and shook his head, pulled his cotton woven coat tightly around him and turned up his collar; then made his way across the fields to where Mila was waiting for him.

Mila was standing outside her home and next to her, was her mother and other women of the village. As Malic drew closer, he could see that they were all holding garments, cushions and tapestries; all were a myriad of colours and textures and next to Mila's mother, sat a large cushion, which would be used for sleeping on.

Malic came to a halt just outside Mila's house; he was met by Mila, her mother and the women of the village. Mila smiled; her eyes where bright and her smile drove the chills from his spine, leaving only the warmth of Mila's love shining down into his heart. She bowed her head slightly, but Malic reached out and gently raised it again, "You are my queen; it is I who should bow." Malic smiled and tilted his head forward. Her face flushed red and lit up with a shy smile that filled Malic with happiness. Mila's mother came forward and again, Malic bowed his head and bent his knee to show his respect for his mother-to-be. Mila's mother took Mila's hand and joined it with Malic's. This was a tradition; showing that she approved of Malic building a house for her daughter and with this blessing, Malic was free to take Mila to see the house he had built. Malic led Mila by the hand and helped her onto the small, single wooded seat at the front of the cart. Then one-by-one, the women of the village came forward and presented Malic with soft furnishings and tapestries for their home-to-be. There were cushions and throws, curtains and drapes, tablecloths and towels; that all mirrored the colours of the valley. Finally, Mila's mother guided Malic to the cushion that would lie on the bed frame he had made. Malic lifted it, but it was heavy and he stumbled a little as he did. The women giggled but Mila looked on with concern until Malic, winking, lifted it high above his head and onto the cart. Mila smiled and sat down, laughing at Malic's antics. He bowed his head and bent his knee respectfully towards the women of the village then took hold of the reins and led the mule and the cart that carried the love of his life down into the valley, towards what would be their home.

Just before they arrived at the house, Malic stopped the cart and turned to Mila; he looked nervous. Mila looked down at him, "What is it Malic?" she asked. He stepped closer to Mila as she sat on the wooden cart. The sun shone behind her, creating a beautiful silhouette.

"My beautiful Mila, I am a simple man and not a man of wealth. I hope that the house I have built for you is good enough and I hope that I have honoured you enough with my work." Mila reached out her hand and cupped Malic's face,

"My beautiful Malic, the house is a symbol yes, but it is you and your love that brings me here today; not what you have and what you own. It is how you make me feel, it is the way you look into my eyes and the way you care and protect me that makes me love you." Tears of heartfelt happiness welled in Malic's eyes, "You are what stirs my soul and makes my heart swell. No man's wealth can bring true happiness; only sincerity, honesty, kindness and true love can do that." Mila smiled and raised her hand, wiping a single tear from his face that had rolled down his cheek. Malic smiled and Mila smiled back and as she did, the mule pulled forward and started moving towards their house. Mila fell back slightly and screamed out. Malic ran to the mule, grabbed its harness then he turned to look at her to see if she was alright. Mila was giggling and smiling; she called out to Malic, "Maybe he's as excited as me to see our home." Malic grinned with excitement and led the mule towards the house.

As they arrived at the house, the mule and the cart came to a halt. Malic tied the reins to a small tree and turned to Mila, but Mila had already jumped down from the cart and was running towards the house. She ran up the small path that led up to the deck, stopped at the door and then turned towards Malic with excited eyes; as if to ask his permission to enter. Malic looked up at Mila and bowed his head, "Your house my love." Mila, with a smile on her face and her heart racing, slowly pushed open the wooden door and stepped inside the house. Inside, she saw the results of Malic's toil. She stared in wonder at his workmanship and couldn't believe how much he had achieved in such a short time. The walls were made from reddish brown logs from the forest outside and the texture of the bark made the house feel warm and comfortable. She looked up at the roof and wondered how Malic had managed to create such a beautiful house. Her eyes followed the beamed ceiling down to the stove, which caught her gaze. He had fitted the stove in the middle of the wall and she thought it was perfect. She walked towards the door at the back of the house and opened it and as she did, the reflection of the sun on the water shimmered on her face; warming her through. Her heart was full and the smile on her face was constant. She turned back into the house. On the wall in the centre of the room, just behind where Malic was standing, hung the picture of Mila that the boy in the market had drawn. Her eyes filled with tears of joy and she ran to Malic, who caught her in his arms. She held him tight and didn't ever want to let go. Malic put his arms around her and they stood and embraced one another, until Mila lifted her head from Malic's shoulder and looked him in the eyes,

"I am so happy. You have built a house even better than I ever dreamed and Malic if you still want me, I will be your wife." Malic's heart almost burst with joy. His eyes lit up and widened and his smile nearly touched his ears. He took a step back from Mila and punched the air. She laughed as he danced around the room, clapping his hands and laughing. Mila laughed louder still and Malic whooped with joy. He approached Mila and took her hands and together, they laughed and danced around the room. Malic was so happy that Mila had accepted his gift of a house and would soon be his wife. In that moment, Malic couldn't imagine a life without his Mila.

That day, Malic and Mila dressed the house with the beautiful gifts from the women of the village. It had now been transformed into a home, awash with colour. Mila had lit candles and an oil burner that filled the house with the fragrance of fresh lavender from the valley and when they had finished, they stood back and admired what was to be their new home. They smiled at each other and giggled playfully at what they saw. Mila still couldn't believe how lovely the house was and Malic admired how she had transformed a simple wooden house into a beautiful home. The night had drawn in and the light was fading fast so they left the house and made their way to the cart. Malic strapped the harness onto his old mule whilst Mila climbed into the seat. He then led the mule and the cart back to the village and when they arrived at Mila's house, he helped her down, "Thank you so much. I feel like it is all a dream. My heart is full and I cannot wait until we are married so that we can live together in the valley in our new home. Malic held Mila, not wanting to let her go. In the background, Mila's mother had been watching from the house. The sight of Malic and Mila so in love, filled her with joy and she remembered her own lost love. Mila's mother called out to her; ending her embrace with Malic. As she pulled back, she looked deep into Malic's eyes and said "Malic, I love you." She meant it with all that she was and Malic knew it. He could feel her love pierce his heart and it filled him with happiness. Mila walked away, but before she entered her house, she turned and smiled at Malic and now he knew what true love felt like.

"Meet me at the house tomorrow," he said. Mila nodded and smiled then turned, walked into the house and closed the door behind her.

A great storm

Malic made his way home. The air was cold and the cool breeze had now turned into a blustery wind. Malic climbed onto the cart and made his way to the stables at the bottom of the field. The wind started to howl and as it blew, it rattled the doors of the stable. He got down from the cart and opened the stable door but as he did, the wind caught it and slammed it open against the entrance to the barn. He grabbed the reins of his old mule and led it into the, now shaking, barn. He then stepped back outside and battled the wind to close the stable door. Rain had started to fall and the noise on the tin roof of the stable grew louder by the second; it was as though the season had changed within an instant and Malic was glad that he finished his house before the coming of the storms.

Malic took off the mule's harness and hung it on the wall. He then went over to a haystack in the corner of the stable and spread fresh hay on the floor for his mule and filled the bucket from a barrel of rain water, which was starting to fill fast. The wind blew harder and the stable doors rattled louder. There was a storm fast approaching and Malic knew he had to get home. He left the stable and shut the door behind him. It was dark and just above the mountain, the sky lit up with a blue flash of lightning. Malic hurried through the village as thunder started to rumble and the lightning became more frequent; lighting up the sky and the mountain every time it struck. When he arrived, the house was empty. Malic called out for his father, but there was no answer. He looked into his father's bedroom, but he wasn't there. Malic was worried as the storm outside was getting fiercer with every moment, and although his father was an experienced shepherd, the mountain was no place for any man during a storm. Malic paced up and down when suddenly, a large crash of thunder caused him to wince and duck his head. He felt afraid and hoped that his father had sought shelter from the storm on his way back down the mountain. Then a loud knock on the door shocked Malic; his heart raced. He went to the door and opened it; it was Jafkin. The lightning cracked and lit up the sky and Malic stood back, "What do you want?" he asked Jafkin.

"Malic, it's your father…." Malic was taken aback by what he said and the shock of Jafkin coming to his house dissipated as his words filtered through to him.

"What about my father?" he asked. Jafkin stepped inside the house and closed the door. Malic was wary of Jafkin and wondered why he had come to his house; after all, it was only a few short weeks ago that he and Jafkin had come to blows. Jafkin spoke,

"Malic, your father visited my house today to thank my father and to seek my apology; but something has happened." Malic moved forward towards Jafkin,

"What about my father?" he asked in a stark manner "He was at my father's house and was taken ill. My father told me to come and bring you to be with him." Malic's heart sank at the thought of losing his father and he froze for a moment. He then rushed towards the door to make his way to Jafkin's father's house. As he was leaving, Jafkin shouted to him, "Take my horse; it will get you there faster. Hurry!" Jafkin urged. Malic ran out of the door and into the storm. He ran up to Jafkin's horse, untethered and mounted it and charged off into the night. Jafkin stood for moment with his eyes closed then slowly he opened them and as he did, an evil smile crept across his face.

Mila was sitting in her house with her mother in front of the fireplace; both had large blankets draped over their laps, and Mila's mother had just placed another log onto the fire and sat back. She looked over to Mila and spoke, "The storms have arrived." Mila looked frightened and lifted her feet up under the blanket. "The valley is a beautiful place and the mountain does all it can to protect us from them, but many people of the village have been taken away by the storms in the night." Mila thought back and saw herself as a little girl, when her mother sat by her bed and comforted her whilst a storm raged outside. She shuddered as she remembered how her tear-faced mother cradled her in her arms and held her close. She couldn't remember exactly what had happened, but after that particular night, she never saw her father again. Mila's mother sighed and looked at her, "He is a good man," she said.

"Who?" replied Mila.

"Malic." The cold feeling that had crept into her heart warmed, as she thought of Malic. Her mother continued, "I think we need to start to make plans for your wedding." Mila's heart leapt with joy,

"Oh Mother, I'm so happy. I can't wait to marry Malic and I can't wait to show you the house he has built for us." Mila's mother smiled,

"Now Child, why don't you make us some tea and we will talk about it." Mila stood up and hugged her mother tight then took the pot from next to the fire and walked over to the water bucket that stood by the door. She was just about to fill the pot when the front door crashed open. It was Jafkin. She screamed as Jafkin slammed the door behind him. Mila dropped the pot and ran behind her mother's chair. Her mother sat upright as Jafkin raised his hands; palms outstretched,

"No, I mean you no harm. It's Malic…" Mila's breathing seemed to stop mid-flow. Jafkin continued, "Malic's father was caught in the storm on the mountain and my father's men and Malic have gone to rescue him. Malic was injured and he was calling for you Mila. My father sent me here to take you to him." Mila's heart filled with fear and her eyes welled with tears; she tried to speak, but nothing would come out. Jafkin grabbed the blanket from the chair where Mila had been sitting, held it up and gestured to her, "Come Mila, I must take you to him, before it's too late." Mila hesitated, but Jafkin insisted, "Mila I mean you no harm, I have loved you just as much as Malic; I am doing this for you." Mila's mother sat back in her chair and looked at her, then nodded her approval. Mila stepped forward and Jafkin wrapped her in the blanket and led her to the door. "You will have to ride with me; it will be faster," he said as they went out into the storm.

The wind was blowing and the rain was lashing down onto the muddy pathways of the village, creating an ever-growing stream of water. Jafkin had a second horse tied up to Mila's fence; he helped Mila up onto his horse and mounted it himself. He dug his heels in hard and the horse galloped away. Immediately Mila noticed that instead of heading to the mountain path, they were riding into the valley. She shouted out, "Jafkin where are you going, the mountain is that way?" but Jafkin forced his heels harder into his horse and rode faster through the driving rain. Mila held on tight, too frightened to let go. The sky was awash with lightning as it crackled across the sky and the valley was starting to flood. It was then she saw the house that Malic had built, ahead. Jafkin rode on faster and made his way up the small trail and stopped at the door to the house. He jumped down from the horse and grabbed Mila by the arm; dragging her out of the saddle. He pulled her into the house and threw her to the floor then walked over to the lantern that was on the table and lit it. He hung it on the wall and went back over to Mila.

"Now," he said through gritted teeth, "why don't we finish what we started all those years ago." Mila screamed; her scream mingled with the crack of lightning and the crashing of thunder as she did.

Malic rode through the storm and through the marketplace, up to the house of Josiah. He jumped down from his saddle and ran up to the great house that stood at the top of the steps that led to a set of huge doors. He pushed the doors open and ran inside. There, he saw his father and Josiah sitting in front of a great fire; eating and drinking wine. Malic was confused. "Malic, what is it, is everything alright?" Malic walked slowly towards his father.

"But Jafkin said you had been taken ill." his father stood up,

"Jafkin?" asked his father; now just as confused as Malic, "we haven't seen Jafkin. After coming to see Josiah, we thought it better that we rekindle our friendship and as the storm had come in, Josiah kindly invited me to stay and eat with him." Malic stood and then a wave of realisation ran through his body, "Mila!" he shouted. Malic turned and ran out of the house. His father and Josiah followed after him; only to see Malic get on his horse and ride off into the storm.

"Quick!" Josiah shouted out to his servant. "Fetch me the horses." Josiah led Malic's father out to the stables.

Malic rode hard. The thunder crashed and the rain drove sideways, but he pressed on. The road had become flooded by the time he reached Mila's house. He pushed open the door and Mila's mother stood there in shock, "Malic, but I thought you were trapped on the mountain?" Malic's heart sank. He approached Mila's mother and held her gently by the shoulders,

"Where is she?" Mila's mother realised the same as Malic, that Jafkin had lied.

"It was Jafkin, he took her. He said he was taking her to you, as you were trapped in the storm." Malic held his head in his hands for a moment,

"Did you see which way they went?" Malic pleaded in desperation.

"No, he just took her and left." Malic ran out of the house and got back onto his horse. The horse lifted its front legs and twisted around, and as it landed again, Malic noticed hoof prints in the mud. They were pointing towards the valley. As Malic's horse strode off and jumped the fence into the valley, Josiah and Malic's father arrived on horseback and followed, chasing after him.

Mila sat cowering on the floor as Jafkin approached her. The lightning filled the room every few seconds; outlining Jafkin's dark silhouette. He threw off his robe and walked towards Mila spitting out his next words in anger, "I should have done this many years ago." Mila scrambled to her feet and ran for the door, but Jafkin ran after her and grabbed her by the arm. She reached out and took hold of Malic's crook that he had left next to the door and struck Jafkin in the face with it. He fell to the floor. Mila opened the door and the rain hit her hard in the face nearly blinding her. The valley was flooding and Mila could see Malic and his father heading towards her, riding as fast as they could. She held onto the rail of the deck and started to make her way down towards the valley. Just then, Jafkin ran out of the house and grabbed her. He spun her round and looked into her eyes. Malic was close and he could see Jafkin holding Mila. His teeth gritted with anger and his heart raced as he sped faster towards her. Behind him, his father and Josiah raced to catch up. Jafkin looked up and saw Malic then looked down at Mila and smirked, "If you won't be mine then you won't be anyone's." Jafkin pushed her through the wooden rails that surrounded deck. She fell off the plateau and into the valley. Her head cracked as it hit a large rock below and Mila was knocked unconscious. The water of the flooding valley rushed over her limp, lifeless body. Malic screamed as he saw Mila hit the ground; he raced up to her and jumped down off his horse into the water that was now flowing hard. He picked Mila up and held her in his arms. Jafkin's father and Josiah arrived and whilst Malic's father stopped beside his son, Josiah galloped up to the house and stopped where Jafkin stood. He got off his horse and struck his son across the face; dropping him to his knees,

"Don't you move Boy."? Josiah shouted in anger at him. Jafkin pulled himself into a ball as Josiah looked out from the deck. Malic was sitting in the water with Mila in his arms. He looked into his love's beautiful eyes as she opened them.

"Malic," she said, "I love you." With that, her eyes closed and Malic felt her last breath leave her body. The sky lit up with a crack of lightning and a crash of thunder filled the air. Malic screamed whilst his father stood behind him, with his hands on his son's shoulders. Malic looked up at Josiah, whose face was full of shame and then he turned his attention to Jafkin,

"Why?" he shouted, "why?" but Jafkin was now slumped against the wall of the house with his head in his hands. Malic stood and turned to his father; passing Mila into his arms. He then ran up the trail to the house and towards Jafkin. Death was in his hands and he wanted to hand it to Jafkin. As he ran towards him, Jafkin's father stopped him. Josiah stood in front of Malic and held him back. He wanted to let him pass, but he knew that more death would not make the situation any better. Malic struggled, but Josiah was a big man and he held Malic firm whilst taking hits to the face and chest. "Why? Why?" Malic continually shouted out to Jafkin, who was still holding his head in shame with tears running from his eyes. Malic was exhausted and fell at the feet of Josiah. Josiah rested his hands on Malic's head in pity for him; for he too knew the pain of losing the one he loved. Josiah turned to Jafkin and scorned him.

"Jafkin, you are no son of mine, I want you to get on that horse and leave this village now and never return. You are banished forever and never again call me Father. You are no longer welcome here." Jafkin stood and tried to speak, but Josiah roared, "Go! Leave now and never return, for if you do, it will be I who will be seeking forgiveness for the death of my own son. Now go!" Jafkin ran down the trail past Malic's father, who was still holding Mila's body in his arms, and jumped onto his horse. He looked up at Josiah, but Josiah turned away in shame. Jafkin rode off into the dark of the night. Malic's father approached Malic and Josiah and knelt down, laying Mila at the foot of Josiah; next to Malic. Malic leant over her and sobbed. He held Mila's body tight against his chest. The rain stopped and in the distance, a wolf howled and the haunting sound echoed through valley.

Mila's Spirit

Two days had passed since Mila's death and Malic hadn't moved from the house. He had refused to leave and told his father that he could not face Mila's mother, or the people of the village. He blamed himself for Mila's death and felt he had failed her mother. Malic was lying on the bed in the house and in his hands he clutched the drawing of Mila tight against his chest. Malic's heart felt empty and sadness filled his very soul. Lying on the bed felt like the loneliest place in the world. His mind played out Mila's last scream over and over in his head; the image of her falling, tortured him like a constant nightmare. He was a broken man without her; he felt like a piece of him was missing. He hadn't been able to function and hadn't slept since his beloved Mila had been cruelly taken away by the jealousy that fuelled Jafkin's actions. His blood boiled and anger surged through his veins every time he thought of Jafkin; the cruel images of a desperate man who had taken away all that he had loved, taunted him constantly. The sun was setting and Malic felt like he wanted to fall asleep and never wake up again. Maybe in the darkness, he would find Mila and they could be together again in the afterlife. Malic didn't want to live another second; without Mila his world had been shattered.

As Malic lay on the bed crying tears into the soft cushion Mila's mother had made, the door opened. Malic looked up and called out, "Mila!" his lack of food and sleep had made him delirious. He wiped his eyes and saw that the figure in front of him was that of his father. Malic turned and buried his head into the cushion. His father walked over to him and sat down on the bed. He reached over, placed his hand on the back of Malic's head and gently stroked it. Malic curled himself tighter and squeezed the drawing of Mila close to his chest. His heart fell deeper into the empty blackness, which now replaced the light of love that once shone so bright inside him. The tears of sadness fell from his eyes, like a waterfall of pain and misery. Malic knew he would never feel that love or embrace his beautiful Mila again.

Malic's father took his hand away from his son and a smaller, softer hand replaced it. Malic thought he had felt this touch before and slowly turned around. There, standing next to the bed, was Mila's mother. Malic immediately got up and stood in front of her; her face was old and the lines of life were strewn across it but her eyes reminded him of Mila. Wiping the tears from his eyes as his father looked on, Malic spoke, "I'm so sorry, I failed you and I failed your daughter, I wish I could have saved her life; I should have protected her, forgive me." And with that, Malic fell to his knees crying. Mila's mother reached out her hands, cupped Malic's face and lifted his head. She looked deep into his eyes,

"My beautiful boy, I need not forgive you at all, for you showed my daughter the love and kindness of a true man; you made her the happiest person alive. Malic you made Mila happy, you cared for her and showed her love and she truly loved you too." Malic felt the words of Mila's mother deep within his heart and it comforted him. But against the blackness that had invaded his soul, this small piece of light faded and was quickly replaced with a feeling of loss and emptiness. Knowing that Mila had loved him was both a gift and a curse. Mila's mother asked Malic to stand and he did. When he got to his feet, she led him to the table and his father joined them. Mila's mother sat down and Malic sat opposite. She reached out and took both of his hands into her own and spoke, "Malic, tomorrow we will hold the ceremony for Mila and she will return to the mountain. I understand your pain, I know how much you loved my daughter and as I too feel that pain, I know that seeing her lifeless, will be something you will not want to have in your memories. Malic, I want you to keep all the good memories of Mila in your mind and I want you to try and concentrate on the beauty of love that existed between you both." She held his hands tighter, "Your pain is too great and I know that seeing Mila again without life in her body will only add to that pain. Stay here until after the ceremony, I don't want you to add any more suffering to your already broken heart. It is my wish that your father will be here with you, and I will stay at the ceremony; not because I don't want you to be there, but I want to save you from a memory that will add to your sadness." Mila's mother's words comforted Malic again as he knew that she was right. He could not take the sadness of seeing a lifeless Mila; he wanted to remember her when she smiled sweetly at him and laughed out loud. Malic agreed. Mila's mother leant forward and kissed him on the forehead. She stood and took Malic's father's hand and together; they walked to the front door and out of the house. Before he left, Malic's father pointed to a small carafe of wine he had left on the table,

"To help you sleep," he said. "I will return tomorrow." He then left, gently closing the door behind him. Malic walked over to the table and picked up the carafe of wine. He took a cup from the shelf and filled it then walked over to the bed. Before he sat down, he drank the large cup of wine straight down and instantly, he felt it warm him through. Quickly, he filled the cup again and again; drinking the wine straight down. He then sat on the bed; the wine ran through his veins and immediately, Malic felt a sense of drowsiness hit him. He picked up the drawing of Mila and held it against his chest as he fell back onto the large cushion. His eyes closed and he fell into the empty blackness of sleep.

Malic winced as he opened his eyes. The sun shone through a gap in the wall of the house; it created a beautiful dust-filled beam that came to rest on his face. He rubbed both his hands over his face and through his hair. It was then he remembered; this was the day his beautiful Mila's body would be passed on to the mountain. Malic felt frail. He stood up and walked slowly over to the door and out onto the front deck. The sun shone and the sky was blue and in the distance where the village stood, a plume of smoke started to rise into the heavens above. Mila's spirit had been set free unto the mountain. Malic stood with tears rolling down his face. As he looked out across the valley, the love he held for Mila hung heavy in his heart. He yearned for something he knew he could never have; one last conversation with his beloved, one last chance to hold her hand, to hear her giggle one more time and one last sweet kiss. Malic stood and watched the smoke rise and as it rose higher into the sky, sadness became engrained deeper into his soul. Malic could not imagine a life without his Mila, and yet that is all that lay ahead.

Revenge

Malic stood for what seemed like hours, watching the smoke of the fire that took Mila's spirit to the mountain. Eventually the smoke became thinner and finally disappeared. Mila's spirit had passed over to the mountain and he knew that all he had left was a picture that lay on his bed, and the memories inside his mind. Malic stepped back into the house; it no longer felt like a home. Now to him, it was an empty wooden shell. He picked up the picture of Mila and looked deeply into the image that was drawn on it. He traced his finger along the outline of her face, wanting nothing more than to feel her soft skin and smell her sweet perfume. But all he felt was the roughness of the paper. In his mind, all he could think of was Jafkin and how he had taken Mila away. Anger filled his chest and there and then, he screamed out loud; vowing vengeance against the man who had taken her away. In his anger, he screwed up the picture and threw it into the hearth of the fire. His whole body shook with anger and rage. He turned and grabbed the carafe of wine from the table and drank it straight down. The sticky, sweet, burning fluid filled his stomach and he felt the heat of it rush through his whole body. After a large gulp, the wine burned Malic's throat; causing him to stop and cough. The wine ran through his empty stomach and flowed into his blood going straight to his head. He took a deep breath then again, lifted the carafe and took another large gulp. As he did, his father entered the front door and immediately, he walked over to Malic and took the carafe from his hand causing the wine to spurt out the sides of his mouth. Malic looked up at his father, "Give it to me," he shouted angrily.

"Son, this is not the answer." Malic pushed his father backwards and again, shouted at him,

"But it was good enough for you." Malic surged forward towards his father, who looked at Malic shocked. Then his demeanour changed to that of his former, younger, stronger self.

"Malic!" he said sternly; stopping Malic in his tracks. "Stop this now!" Malic felt like a boy again, who was being chastised by his father and he stopped immediately snapping out of his outburst of anger. He stood in front of his father, instantly ashamed of his behaviour. His father held up the carafe and spoke, "This wine may temporarily take away the pain, but if you get lost in it, you will be lost forever." Malic retorted,

"But what do I have left now Father; but heartbreak and pain?" Tears filled Malic's eyes and the anger inside him reared its head once more. "My Mila, my beautiful Mila has been taken from me," he continued through gritted teeth and frothing spittle, "That man, that jealous horrible excuse for a man took her away from me." His father reached out and placed his hands on Malic's shoulders,

"What is it you want Malic, revenge? Don't you think there has been enough death?" Malic turned away from his father and paced the room,

"No! One death would not be enough for him, he deserves a thousand deaths." His father walked towards him,

"My boy, do you not understand? If you seek revenge, then you become just like him. Malic it is a time to grieve, not a time for revenge." Malic rubbed both his hands through his hair, pulled down his head and bent over; as if in pain.

"But Father, how can I let Jafkin get away with taking the life of the woman I love?" His father moved closer to him, put his arm around him then walked him over to the bed and sat him down.

"Son, the spirit of the mountain is a powerful force that creates balance in life." He spoke softly, "Sometimes, we have to let the walk of life take its own path, and understand that there is always a price to pay when our intentions are bad and our deeds are malicious. Malic, no man can take the life of another and not pay the price, but it is not you who has to be collector of that debt; that Malic, is a debt for the universe to collect." Malic's head fell into his father's lap and he stroked it to comfort him. Together they sat there until Malic eventually fell asleep.

Later that evening Malic awoke, and as he opened his eyes he saw two silhouettes standing in the doorway. He sat up when he recognised the voice of Josiah and instantly, anger filled his chest. He got up from the bed and walked quickly over to the door. His father put his hand across the doorway; stopping him from getting to Josiah, "What is he doing here?" Malic said angrily." Josiah raised his hands and bowed his head slightly,

"Malic!" his father shouted, "be quiet!" Again, like a small boy being told off by his father, he stopped as Josiah spoke,

"Malic, I have come to give you my apologies and offer you my help; if there is anything I can do, please tell me." From behind his father's outstretched arm, Malic, with malice in his eyes and fire in his breath, answered Josiah,

"What is it you can offer me that can replace what was taken by your son? What could you ever do to replace what I have lost? Your son took the life of the woman I was going to marry, and you think you can replace her with gifts, money and apologies?" Josiah took a step back,

"Malic, I understand how you feel, I just wanted to try and do what I could for you." Malic moved closer; leaning over his father's arm which was braced across the doorway,

"Can you bring my Mila back?"

Josiah's head fell in shame, "No! I didn't think you could. You don't know my pain, you don't know what I am going through, and you don't know what it is like to have the life of someone you love, taken away in front of your very eyes. You don't know the pain of not being able to do anything, whilst the life of the one you love slips away." Malic's father's head fell and Josiah bowed his head further,

"Maybe Malic, I know more about that pain that you think." With this, Josiah nodded to Malic's father and stepped away from the door; revealing behind where Josiah stood, a tree in the valley, right next to the spot where Mila had died and from the branches of the tree, hung Jafkin. Malic's father lowered his arm and Malic stepped outside onto the deck. He looked down into the valley where Josiah was approaching the tree. Underneath the branch that Jafkin's body hung from, was a horse and cart. Josiah stepped onto the back of the cart, pulled out a large knife and took hold of his son's body and then cut the rope that Jafkin hung by. His limp body fell into his father's arms as Malic looked on. Josiah laid his son on the straw-laden cart then took the seat at the reins of the horse and slowly pulled off. As he did, he bowed his head in the direction of Malic. Malic breathed out heavily and then slowly bowed his head in return. He regretted not listening to Josiah; he understood that Jafkin's actions were not of Josiah's making and now Josiah, like him, would have to grieve the loss of someone he loved. Malic turned and walked back into the house and his father closed the door. He walked over to his son and said,

"Josiah is an honourable man and respected your grief above his own. Malic, there has been enough death in this valley and now it is time to grieve." Malic again laid his head on his bed and cried himself to sleep, as his father sat by his side.

Lost

The next morning, Malic awoke with the warmth of the sun shining on his face and through a sunray that lit up the falling dust in the room; he saw a silhouette of a person standing bathed in the light, “Mila” he called out. He rubbed his eyes and the silhouette came into focus; it was his father. Malic's heart sank as the realisation of losing Mila hit his heart again. He sat up and his father handed him a bowl of soup,

“Malic, you must eat.” but Malic turned and laid his head back down onto the cushion on which he lay. “Malic please, you must eat. You cannot let your grief ruin your health.” Malic heard his father’s words but took no notice; he didn't want to eat. He just lay in silence thinking of the love he had lost. His father placed the soup on the table, “Malic, I have to go and tend to the herd; I will leave this here for you. You must eat. I will return later.” And with this, Malic's father kissed him on the back of the head and left. Malic lay on the bed for a short while until eventually he slowly got up. He walked past the food and went to the cupboard where the wine he had drunk was kept. On opening the cupboard, he found it was empty. Malic looked around the house for the carafe, but it had gone. He realised that his father had taken it, to ensure he did not get drunk again that day. Malic's spirits were low and he felt empty inside; he felt like there was no point to his life now he was alone. He sat down but all he could see in his mind's eye was the image of his beautiful Mila, lying lifeless in his arms. He tried so hard, yet could not block out the pain and heartache he was feeling inside; but he knew that the wine he drank the night before could. Malic dressed in his linen trousers and pulled on a hooded tunic. He pulled up the hood, took the few coins he had left from the box his father had given him, left the house and made his way to the market. When he arrived, he found that the hustle and bustle of the market that once filled him with excitement had gone. The noise of the traders' calls hurt his head and the smell of the spice made him feel sick to his stomach. The sounds of the traders shouting and selling their wares annoyed him. The square no longer seemed like a magical place to be and he just wanted to be alone. But before that, Malic needed to buy more of the wine that had helped him block out the pain he felt inside. Malic approached a market trader who was selling wine. He asked the trader for his strongest; the trader obliged and poured him a small cup of wine. Malic drank it straight down; the strength of it took his breath away but instantly, the familiar warmth that followed comforted him. Malic took out the coins and handed them to the trader, "Give me as many carafes as this money will buy." The trader took the coins and counted them then took down twelve carafes of wine and placed them on a table in front of him. The trader then picked up a large sack and filled it with the carafes and handed it to Malic. Malic lifted the heavy sack and made his way back home. As he reached the valley, he sat down to rest. He took one of the carafes from the sack and drank from it. He drank a small amount at first, but after he felt the warmth of it flow through his chest, he raised the carafe up and drank deep from it. The strong wine soon reached his head; making it numb. Malic stood and started to walk back to the house, constantly sipping from the carafe as he went.

By the time he reached his house, his vision was blurred and his legs were weak. He started to climb the path up to his house and as he did, he fell; the wine had taken hold and Malic was drunk. Every time he tried to get back to his feet, he fell again. Eventually, Malic stopped trying to get up and sat in the middle of the path. He sat and drank the last few drops from the carafe and as he did, his head fell to the floor. Looking up into the clouds, the world spun; his eyes closed and he fell deep into unconsciousness.

A few hours later, Malic awoke to the patter of raindrops hitting his face. He sat up and as he did, a pain ran right through his head making him wince as he got to his feet. His mind was clouded and his body was still full of the effects of the wine but he picked up the sack and slowly stumbled towards the house. When Malic reached the house, he fell through the door and the carafes fell out of the sack; one of them broke and leaked the wine all over the floor. He scrambled to save it but it was too late; it had soaked into the rug and was gone. He reached out to take hold of the carafe and as he did, he blacked out again.

When Malic eventually awoke, it was dark and the house was cold. His head felt numb at first until he stood up then again, a searing pain hit him. Malic got to his feet and went over to the door. He didn't want to see anyone and with this in mind, he pulled across the heavy bolt he had fashioned to lock the door then went over and sat on the bed. His mind was still clouded and all he could feel was the sadness that filled his heart. He reached out and took hold of a carafe of wine; he couldn't face the pain any longer and turned to the wine to help him forget. Once again he drew long and deep from the carafe and again, he blacked out into unconsciousness.

The next day Malic awoke to a loud banging on the door; he opened his eyes, but his vision was blurred and all he could see was the hazy light of the morning seeping in through the walls of the house. Malic's father shouted out, "Malic, are you in there?" Malic lay on the bed not wanting to answer. His father called out again, "Malic, this is not the way, please Son, open the door." Malic curled up into a ball; he didn't want to face the world without his Mila. Once more, Malic's father called out, "Malic come, please open the door." Malic reached out and pulled the blanket from underneath him; up and over his head. He put his hands over his ears and blocked out the sound of his father's voice until eventually, there was silence; Malic's father had left. Malic lay under the blanket for hours; he knew he couldn't face the day. As he lay reminiscing about the days he spent walking with Mila in the valley, tears fell from his eyes and in the dark, a deep sadness engulfed him.

'How can I live without her?' he thought. 'What is the point of my life now? How can I go on?' The thoughts spun around in his head constantly and he knew the only thing that could stop them, was the wine. Malic got up from under the cover and again, took a carafe of wine and drank from it. As he drank, the sadness engulfed him more, but he couldn't stop. He knew that once the effects of the sweet, sticky liquor took effect, he would be oblivious to all his feelings. Malic drank constantly that day; he wanted to just fall asleep and never wake up. He could not see a life without his Mila.

Over the next few days this continued; Malic being awoken by his father banging on his door and him hiding away from the world, lost to the blackness that the wine brought him. Then one day, the banging stopped and no one came.

Malic awoke early before the sun had risen. He reached out for the wine but the last carafe was empty. He got up and walked over to the box where he kept his coins; inside the box was a single coin. He took it out then swiped the box off the table, shattering it. Thoughts of Mila entered his head; the image of her falling from the deck taunted him and Malic knew the only way he could block out these cruel images, was with more of the wine. He looked around the room for something he may be able to trade. It was then, he heard the braying of his mule coming from outside. Without washing, he put on his sandals and made his way outside. Malic untied his mule and led it through the valley to the market.

When he arrived at the wine trader's stall, he asked the trader how much of the wine the single coin would buy him. The trader took the coin and gave malic two carafes of wine. Malic asked for more but the trader refused, "Surely I have enough for more than two?" Malic pleaded, but the trader said not and two would be all the coin would buy. Malic got angry with the trader and moved in close to him. "Two is not enough, I need more!" The trader became defensive and stood his ground,

"No coins; no wine," the trader said. In his anger Malic went to push the trader but he moved and Malic fell to the ground. "Would you like me to call a guard?" the trader asked Malic who was now sitting on the floor looking up at him. He knew that the market guards were Josiah's men and that would lead to Josiah informing his father of his whereabouts. Malic pulled himself to his feet and slowly approached the trader with his hands outstretched,

"Forgive me," said Malic, "I just need to have more wine. Can you not spare me just one more?" The trader looked at him in his desperation then turned and looked at Malic's Mule,

"Your mule; I will trade you two barrels for your mule." Malic stood for a moment and thought. He looked at the mule and asked himself what use would his mule be now anyway? He agreed to the trader's offer. He knew he would never need his old mule again; for he had planned to drink himself to the end. Malic just wanted to sleep forever. The trader called out to his son and told him to take the mule to his stable, then get two barrels of wine and take them to Malic's home. Malic bowed his head to the trader and with the two carafes in his hands he followed the trader's son to their stables.

When he arrived at the trader's stable, the boy tied up Malic's old mule and loaded a cart with two barrels of wine. He got onto the cart and signalled Malic to get into the back, which he did. They left the stable and drove through the market and as they did, they passed the stall of Tobias. Malic's heart sank as he remembered the green stone that Tobias gave him as a gift for Mila. In shame, he hid behind the two barrels of wine; he didn't want Tobias to see him in his drunken state. He sat back and drank from one of the carafes of wine whilst the boy led the horse and cart out of the village to his home.

Again that night and every night that followed, Malic filled his carafe from the barrel and drank from it. But now, he had to drink more and more to fall into the blackness that he so welcomed. He would get so drunk that sometimes, he would forget why he was even drinking and would curse the world. One night, whilst shouting at nothing in particular, his father banged on the door and asked if he was in the house. Malic shouted out in anger, "Yes."

"It's me, your father." Malic could hardly walk and stumbled over to the door,

"Go away!" he shouted.

"Malic, I need to see you. You cannot go on like this, hiding away and drinking away your life." Malic laughed a cynical laugh,

"What life? I have no life." Malic's father replied,

"But Malic, there are people who love you, I love you; it doesn't have to be this way." Malic leant his forehead against the wooden door; he was so full of wine, he could hardly stand up. He spoke, but his father could not hear him so he too leant his forehead against the door. The wooden door was the only thing that separated their heads from touching. Malic's father spoke softly, "Malic, please come home, this is not what Mila would have wanted. Open the door and I will take you home with me." Malic listened to his father for a moment. A strange calmness came over him; he knew his father's intentions were good. He stood leaning against the door for a moment then replied,

"Home? Home you say. This was meant to be my home. This empty house was meant to be our home, we were to have children and live our lives together here in this house." Malic's father felt the sadness of his son in his own heart. He understood what it was to be lonely; now his wife had passed on to the spirit of the mountain.

"Malic, I know the pain of loneliness," his father said, "I know how it must feel for you, but please Malic, losing yourself in that wine is not the answer. Please open the door and I will help you." There was a silence then Malic became angry,

"You know my pain? I doubt that very much Father. Shouldn't you be consoling your friend Josiah? Remember him? The man you sat with whilst his son planned to kill my Mila." Malic's father's heart sank as Malic grew angrier, "Why don't you go and see if Josiah is well. After all, isn't he your friend?" Malic punched the door and his father stood back. He could hear Malic's rage through the door; all he wanted to do was help his son and console him, but Malic continued, "Go! Go away and do not return, go and sit with your friend Josiah. Maybe he needs consoling after the death of his poor Jafkin." At this, Malic kicked and threw the furniture around the house. All the things he had worked for and bought from the market, he broke. He threw the chairs and turned the bed upside down. He pulled down the cupboard and kicked the table across the kitchen and as he did, he fell and banged his head on the hearth of the fire. His father shouted through the door,

"Son, are you alright? Son, talk to me." There was a silence then Malic called out,

"Father go away and never come back. I don't want to come home and I don't want to talk to you. Go and see your friend Josiah." His father knew there was no more he could say and with tears falling from his face, he made his way down the pathway, onto his horse and home.

Inside the house, Malic lay with his head next to the hearth; blood seeped from a small cut above his eye. He searched for something to wipe it; his vision was blurred and his body was tired. He reached out and took hold of the first thing he touched. He pulled it towards him and as he went to wipe his brow, he saw what is was. It was the portrait of Mila from the market he had thrown into the fireplace. Malic looked at the outline of his beautiful Mila; the feeling of loss tore his heart apart and tears fell from his eyes as he clasped the picture against his chest. The sadness and the pain were like never before. That night Malic slept on the floor, holding the last remnant of his true love close to his heart.

Tobias's advice

It had now been weeks since Malic's father had last visited him and although he thought about him every day, he couldn't bring himself to see his only son killing himself with wine. He blamed himself for introducing Malic to it, but he thought at the time it was normal, as all the fathers in the village would take a first drink with their sons; it was tradition. Malic's father made his way to market to fetch supplies. With Malic not being around, it was getting harder for him to tend to his flock and work the fields. Today he would go to market and seek to employ help until, he thought, Malic would see sense and return home. Although Malic was lost; his father had hope. When he reached the market, he asked a trader if he knew of anyone who would want to be employed and help him work his fields. The trader told him to go to the jewellery quarter of the market and find a trader called Tobias. Tobias always knew whom to contact for all manner of things. Malic's father thanked the trader and made his way through the bustling market to the stall of Tobias. When he arrived at Tobias's stall Tobias greeted him,

"Hello, my friend. How may I help you?"
Malic's father spoke,

"I was told that you might know of someone to help me work my fields. My son has left my home and with me having to tend to my herd and reap this year's harvest alone, the work has become too much." Tobias invited Malic's father into the back of his stall and sat him down. He poured tea into two cups and handed one to Malic's father.

"Tell me, what has happened to your son?" He sighed and then spoke,

"My son has lost his wife and since then, has done nothing but hide away and drink wine. He stays in his house and never comes out; his heart is broken and his soul has become lost in drunkenness." Tobias had heard of what happened in the valley and realised that the man sat before him was Malic's father.

"I am sorry to hear of what has happened and I will help." Tobias stood up and went out of the stall and after a few moments came back with a young, strong-looking man. "This is Emile. He will help you tend to your fields; he is a good worker and will stay with you until your son returns." Malic's father stood up and shook Tobias's hand,

"Thank you. I will pay him well and feed him and there is a room at my house where he can stay whilst he works for me. As for my son, I think all hope is lost; I haven't seen him for such a long time and I doubt that he will ever want to see me again." Tobias held on to Malic's father's hand and spoke softly,

"There are greater forces in this universe than you and I. Do not lose hope; keep it in your heart and your prayers will be answered." With that Malic's father left with Emile, and made his way home. Tobias sat and finished his tea and thought about Malic and the pain he must be feeling. He decided that that night, he would go to the valley and visit him.

Later that night, Tobias gathered some tea, spices, fruit, vegetables and meat and packed them into the saddlebags of his horse. Then he took some ointment and placed that into a bag he wore on his side. He mounted his horse and rode into the valley and up the path to Malic's house. Malic was lying on his bed, when there was a knock at his door. He ignored it until the knock became louder and Tobias called out. "Malic, it is I; Tobias." Malic wasn't expecting to hear the voice of Tobias and it shocked him. He sat up on his bed and stared across the room at the door. He called out again, "Malic, open the door, I need to speak with you." Malic looked around the room and felt ashamed as the house was untidy and the broken furniture that he had thrown across the room was still upturned. The house smelt of wine and dust, he hadn't eaten or washed and his hair and his beard had grown long. In that moment,

Malic realised that he had become nothing more than a man surviving on wine, heartache, sadness and pain.

"Please leave me alone." Malic shouted out. "I have nothing for you." Malic heard Tobias laugh.

"My boy, I want nothing from you, all I want to do is talk to you. You do remember me don't you? I am the man who gave you Mila's necklace. Why should I want anything from you?" Malic knew the instant he heard the voice, who was at the door, but didn't want to acknowledge it to be him. The thought of Tobias seeing him like this filled him with shame. Once more, Tobias called out, "I will not leave. I can stand here all night, so you may as well open the door and let me speak; besides, if after I have spoken, you want to lock yourself up in this prison, you can." Tobias's words made Malic realise, that the house he once built to become a home for him and Mila, had become just that; a prison of sadness. Malic stood up and approached the door. He stood for a moment, and then lifted the bar that held it shut and opened it. Tobias greeted him with a smile, "May I?" he said, gesturing towards the door. Malic stood back and Tobias entered the house. He looked around the dark room and at Malic, "Well, you seem to have forgotten which way up the furniture goes," he said in a jovial voice. He walked over to the table and turned it the right way up then pulled two chairs to the table and invited Malic to sit with him. Malic sat down at the table opposite Tobias. Tobias looked Malic up and down, "What have you done Malic, what have you become? You've lost weight." Malic lowered his head in shame then Tobias placed his hand under Malic's chin and raised it up again. "Malic, you have become lost. I know your heart is heavy and I know that you have lost the most precious thing a man can have; you have lost the one you love. But you cannot live like this anymore." A tear fell from Malic's eye; he knew that Tobias was a good man and he wanted nothing more than to help him. Tobias continued, "Malic, when did you last go to the mountain?" Malic spoke but his voice was weak,

"I have never been to the mountain," he replied.

"Never?" said Tobias.

"No," Malic replied, "I have always been told to stay away from the mountain because of the black wolf." Tobias took his hand away from Malic's face and sat back with his legs crossed,

"Malic now is the time; you need to go to the mountain. Although the black wolf does live in the mountain, there is also great good there. The mountain is a fountain of both good and bad, but what is held in your heart, determines what you will find there. Malic I want you to go there and call out to the spirit of the mountain; it is there where you will find your answers." Malic looked at Tobias and around the house that was strewn with old empty carafes and broken furniture. He looked at the barrels of wine that were now empty and inside, he cursed himself for what he had let himself become. It was in this moment, he knew that Tobias was right and he couldn't continue living like this. Malic agreed that the next morning, he would leave his house and seek out the spirit of the mountain. Tobias stood up and went outside, he bought in the two saddlebags he had laden with goods and placed them on the floor by the door. "This is for you Malic; I have a feeling you might need it." Tobias walked over to Malic and embraced him. "Tomorrow at the mountain, do not fear the black wolf; if you call out to the spirit with an open heart, you will be answered." Tobias then handed him two bottles from out of his bag; one was oil of lavender, the other, a clear liquid he had never seen before, "Take these. This one," Tobias pointed to the lavender, "it will help you sleep; put some of it on the hot hearth before you got to bed." Then he pointed to the other bottle and said, "This will heal your hands." Malic looked at the bottle then back at Tobias,

"But my hands are fine." he replied. Tobias smiled a knowing smile, "Yes they are; for now," and with that Tobias left. Malic stood at the door and watched Tobias ride off out of the valley, against the shadow of the mountain that stood in the distance. When he was out of sight, Malic closed the door and went back into his house. He walked over to the fireplace and picked up the portrait of Mila then walked over to the bed and lay down; holding her picture in his arms until he fell asleep.

The Mountain

The next morning Malic awoke, still holding the picture of Mila. He stood up and looked at her face that was etched onto the paper; his heart was heavy. He walked over to the fireplace and pinned the picture to the nail in the wall where it used to hang. He turned and walked out of the door and looked out to the mountain in the distance. The sun shone bright and Malic knew that today, he would go to the mountain and call out to the spirit. He didn't know what to expect but he knew Tobias was a good man who had nothing but good intention for him; so he decided to trust Tobias and set off into the valley. Malic walked for hours; the sun was high in the sky and eventually he reached the mountain and started to climb up higher and higher. His mind was on the black wolf, but he didn't care if today was the day he would lose his life because, if today was his day to leave the miserable existence he was leading then so be it. He pressed on; today he would do as Tobias asked and call out to the spirit of the mountain.

After hours of climbing, Malic reached a small clearing at the edge of a cliff, near the top of the mountain. He was exhausted and sat for a moment; his heart was beating out of his chest, he knew that this was the territory of the black wolf and it scared him. Every ounce of Malic's spirit was telling him to leave this place and to go back down the mountain. His mouth was dry and his body ached but he knew inside, this was where he was meant to be. The clouds hung low against the blue sky and the air was thin. Malic tried to call out, but his throat was dry and no words left his mouth. On the edge of the cliff was a small tree and the mist from the mountain had gathered in its leaves; creating little pools of water. Malic approached the tree to drink the water that had gathered in its leaves, but as he did, he heard a growling coming from a dark cave just beyond it. He froze; fear filled his soul and then out of the darkness of the cave walked the black wolf. It growled and lowered its head and walked slowly towards Malic. Stalking around him, Malic was frozen to the spot; but followed the wolf with his eyes. Suddenly, the black wolf bared its razor-like teeth and snarled. Malic found it in him to step backwards, until he was teetering on the edge of the cliff. The wolf slowly walked towards Malic. With its demon-like red eyes piercing Malic's own and its teeth bared, the wolf leapt at Malic. It landed on his chest, knocking him to the ground. Malic struggled and held the wolf by its throat. He could feel its claws ripping away at his flesh. Its head turned and bit Malic's fingers from his hand; he screamed in pain. The wolf turned its head; this time, closer to Malic's face. It snarled and bared its teeth again, then bit at his throat. At that moment, Malic realised that he had failed and the wolf was about to take his life. Just as he was expecting death, the words of Tobias rang out inside his head,

'Tomorrow, at the mountain, do not fear the black wolf and if you call out to the spirit with an open heart, you will be answered.'

Malic screamed out, "Spirit, help me!" and suddenly he awoke. Malic was sitting on the rock, by the edge of the cliff. He looked down at his body and at his hands; there was no blood on his hands and no claws had pierced his chest and his fingers were still attached. He stood up and looked around him. It was then that he noticed the silence; the air had become still and the clouds had cleared. Then out of nowhere, Malic heard a voice inside his head. "My son, what is it you seek?" It was the spirit of the mountain. Malic fell to his knees and looked around him. He couldn't see anything except the tree and the blue sky. Inside he felt a calmness like never before. Malic spoke,

"I seek understanding. I want to know why, if you are the spirit of the mountain and you control everything, why did you let my Mila die?"

Malic again looked around him, until the voice in his head spoke,

"My son, life is life and death is death; that is the way of the world. Even I cannot control what lives and what dies." Malic became angry,

"But if you are the great spirit of the mountain, tell me how am I supposed to live now? Why did you give me everything, only to take it all away?" Malic stood up and walked around, looking for the source of the voice in his head; but he only saw the trees and the bushes that stood at the edge of the cliff. Again the voice spoke out inside his head,

"My son, life is life and death is death. If you want to live, then you must honour the woman you loved and one day, you will be together again." Malic looked to the sky for the source of the voice in his head, but all he could see were the birds that hovered above him. He shouted out,

"But what am I to do with the emptiness this death has brought to my life? How can I honour what is no longer living?" For a moment, silence reined then the voice again called out,

"Build yourself a temple, build it strong and build it on a solid foundation and every day, honour your love that is lost; it is then you will be together again." Malic again looked all around him for the source of the voice, but all he saw were the snow-capped mountains standing majestically against the clear blue sky. Malic called out,

"But how can she return? How can I be with her again if she is dead?" Immediately and louder than before, the voice boomed out inside his head,

"BUILD YOURSELF A TEMPLE!"
Suddenly, a strong wind blew and Malic was forced back to the edge of the cliff. He tried to reach out to take hold of the branches of the tree but as he did, the wind whipped up and he was blown backwards off the edge of the mountain. As Malic fell towards the rocks below, images of his life and Mila passed before his eyes and at the moment his body slammed into the rocks below, again he woke up. Once again he found himself sitting on the rock in the clearing on the mountain, in front of the tree. The last words he had heard ran through his mind,

'Build yourself a temple.'

Over and over again, those words ran through his head. Malic stood up; his mouth was dry, but his body no longer ached. It was getting dark and he knew he had to make his way down from the mountain. He walked over to the tree and drank the water from its leaves; it refreshed him. After drinking as much as he could, he made his way back down the mountain, through the valley to his home. When entered the house, he lay on his bed exhausted and immediately he fell asleep.

The Temple

The next morning Malic awoke; feeling different. The words, 'Build yourself a temple,' still ran constantly through his mind. He got up and decided that this was exactly what he would do. Today, he would find a place high above the valley and build a temple in honour of Mila. Malic got out of bed and without thought of washing or eating, took his axe and went in search of a place to build the temple. He walked through the valley and whilst he searched, the words 'In honour of your love,' ran constantly through his mind. Malic knew that to honour Mila, he would have to build a temple that matched the beauty of her soul. Eventually, he came to the place where he and Mila had sat under the moonlit sky; where he had given her the green stone that he hung around her neck. Once again, sadness filled him. The sadness was so deep it nearly stopped him in his tracks, but the words running through his mind grew louder and it urged him on. Malic stopped for just a second; looking at the spot that he a Mila lay. He kissed his hand and laid it on the rock that he and Mila had leant against. He remembered her deep green eyes and her silky olive skin, the sweet smell of her perfume and the velvet touch of her hair. After a moment's reflection Malic turned to walk away and as he did, he spotted a clearing surrounded by trees and rocks high up above the valley; in the side of another, smaller mountain. He made his way up to the clearing and when he reached it, he walked across it to the edge and there, he saw the most beautiful view of the valley he had ever seen.

Looking out into the valley in the distance, he could see the house that he had built for Mila and below him was the spot that he had given her the necklace. In the distance, the mountain stood majestically, protecting the valley. He could see the beauty of the valley in all its glory: it was awash with the colours of the wild flowers that grew there and their scent filled the air. He could see the rich wildlife that lived in the valley; goats and deer grazed in the meadow and high above, eagles soared. The wind blew past the mountain and through the valley causing a symphony of sound for the grass to dance to. Malic knew that this would be the place he would build his temple.

Malic took his axe and went into the trees that surrounded the clearing. He found a great tree that would support the temple he would build and so took his axe and started to hack away at the thick trunk. Malic swung his axe for hours, but still had only chopped half way through the huge trunk. His strength did not last long; his mouth was dry with thirst and he felt weak. He wanted to stop but the words spoken to him on the mountain again ran through his mind,

'Build yourself a temple.'

Malic surged on until eventually the great tree fell, and so did he. As the great tree hit the ground, Malic dropped to his knees with exhaustion. He could work no more that day and after resting for a moment, Malic made his way down into the valley and home.

When he arrived at his house, it wasn't a welcoming sight to see how he had been living. After being out in the fresh air all day, he noticed the stench of the wine permeating from the empty barrels that stood in the corner; the empty carafes that were strewn across the room and the upturned furniture made Malic feel ashamed. Malic decided that that night he would clean the house and make good what he had broken. If he couldn't keep his own home clean, how would he succeed in building a temple? But first Malic needed water. He went outside to the stream and knelt down next to it. He cupped his hands and drank from the cool, fresh spring water that flowed. The water was cold and quickly quenched his thirst. After drinking his fill, Malic scooped up the water in his hands and splashed it over his face; it refreshed him. After drinking from the stream, Malic went back into the house and as he entered the kitchen, he saw the two saddlebags that Tobias had left him. Malic went over to the bags and opened them. Inside, there was fruit, vegetables, fragrant soap, spices and a mirror. Malic put the mirror to one side and took the saddlebags and placed them on the table. He would have put them into the cupboard but the cupboard was lying on the kitchen floor, so Malic bent down and lifted it back into place. Inside was a full carafe of wine that fell out onto the floor. He picked it up and looked at it. The urge to drink the wine was great and he thought about it for a second, but no sooner had he started to think about the welcoming blackness of forgetfulness, the words of the mountain spirit boomed out in his head,

'In honour of your love.'

Malic placed the carafe on the kitchen table. He couldn't bring himself to throw it away, so instead he just pushed it to one side whilst he emptied the saddlebags. Malic filled the cupboard with the food and placed the small mirror face down onto the table. After placing the empty saddlebags in the corner of the kitchen, Malic went back to the cupboard and took out some bread. He was hungry from the day's work and he hadn't eaten for what seemed like an eternity. His body had become thin and frail looking and he was weak. He bit into the bread and relished its flavour. It was just plain bread but it had been so long since he had eaten that to him, it tasted like a banquet in his mouth. After a few mouthfuls Malic's mouth became dry, so he took a cup and went outside and filled it from the stream. Malic then went back into the house and sat at the table, ate the bread and drank the water. He was so tired from the day's work felling the tree that before he finished his bread and water, his head slumped onto the kitchen table and he fell asleep.

When Malic awoke, all that was on his mind was the temple he had to build. The half-eaten piece of bread lay on the table next to the empty cup. It was the middle of the night, it was still dark; too dark to leave the house and build the temple. He sat up at the kitchen table and as he did, he felt every bone in his body creak and ache with pain. It had been such a long time since he had worked as hard as he had that day and swinging his axe had taken it out on his body. Malic stood up slowly and as he did, every muscle and every sinew in his body was racked with pain. He got to his feet and stretched his arms upwards and although it hurt, it also loosened up his tight muscles and eventually the pain subsided. Malic went over to the cupboard and opened it. He reached inside and took out some of the fresh bread and cheese Tobias had brought for him and as he did, in his mind, he thanked Tobias for his gesture of goodwill. Malic took the food over to the table and with a knife, cut a generous slice of the cheese from the large roll then broke some bread; returning the remainder back inside the cupboard. Malic needed to drink and he knew that one small cup would not be enough. He looked around for a larger container for his water but the only thing he could find was the carafe still full of wine. He stood and thought for a moment about drinking the wine inside that had helped him forget so much. But at the same time, he also realised that it was the wine that had made him so weak and had stopped him from feeding his body. Malic took the carafe outside to the stream and opened it. He held it out in front of him. The smell of it was inviting and again he was tempted to drink it but as the thought of drinking the wine entered his mind, an image of the black wolf flashed into his head. The wolf seemed to be smiling and it scared Malic. He shook his head to rid his mind of the image and it disappeared; replaced by the tree on the ledge and a profound silence. Malic instantly knew that the choice he made now would define him and it was the choice he made now, that would determine whether Mila's temple would be built or not. Malic looked at the carafe with hate in his eyes and then turned it upside down, emptying the wine into the moonlit water. The wine mixed with the clear water of the stream and was washed away. He remembered some of his father's words the first time he had drunk the wine, when they sat by the stream behind his father's house. 'What is gone is gone,' and he knew that he had done the right thing. Malic knelt down and washed out the carafe with the water from the stream and filled it. As he did, he felt unburdened. He went back inside the house and sat at the table then ate the cheese and bread and drank the cool, fresh water. The first bite of the cheese tasted strong but beautiful. He could feel it instantly nourishing his body and it felt good. His mouth watered from the creamy, mustardy taste and when he bit into the bread through the hard crust, into the white inner, it felt soft in his mouth and he could taste the earthiness of the flour it had taken to make it. Malic had only eaten half of the bread and a small amount of cheese before he felt full. He hadn't eaten for the last few weeks and his stomach had shrunk, so it didn't take much to fill it. Although it was a simple meal, Malic had never enjoyed one more than this.

After Malic had finished eating, he went about tidying the house. The first thing he did was to throw the empty carafes of wine outside; he knew that to have them inside would only feed his temptation. The vision of the black wolf he had, whilst emptying the first, had scared him; he saw it as a warning. After he came back into the house, he picked up the upturned furniture and straightened it out. He got a cloth from the kitchen and wiped the dust off everything. Then he took a broom and swept through the house. The dust hung in the air; sparkling in the moonlight that beamed in through the open back door. He swept the dust out of the house and into the stream; watching it float away on the top of the water. Under the moonlight, the dust created a shape on the water and for a moment, Malic thought he saw an image of his beloved Mila. It filled him with sadness, but strangely at the same time, he felt himself smile at the vision of her face. As he stood there reminiscing, a cool wind blew and snapped him out of his gaze; Malic hugged himself and rubbed his shoulders to get warm. The cold air had sent a shiver down his spine so Malic decided to light a fire. He cleared the hearth and set about gathering some firewood; he would have to go out into the wood at night and fell a tree to build his fire. He went into the other room and picked up his axe and as he went into the kitchen to get his coat, he walked right past the two empty barrels of wine. Malic stopped and smiled to himself. Minutes later, Malic had dragged the barrels outside and had chopped them both into a pile of wood. The smell of the wine filled his nostrils but this time, the image of the black wolf did not appear in his head, instead he became more determined than ever not to be seduced by the wine again. Malic picked up an armful of the wood and carried it into the house and placed it on the hearth. He then broke some of the pieces down into kindling. Above the fire on the shelf, was a small pot and inside, were a few matches he had bought on his first trip to the market. He took one down and stroked it against the black metal of the fireplace; the match sparked and fizzed into a purple, reddish and eventually yellow flame. The lit match caused a warm glow throughout the kitchen and Malic could feel the warmth of it on his face. It was warmth he needed more than he knew. Malic held the match to the wine soaked wood of the broken barrel; the sticky residue of the wine instantly lit and spread from one piece of kindling to the other. He picked up larger pieces of the wood and placed them carefully on top of the burning kindling; being careful not to smoother the small flames. The pieces ignited quickly and within moments, the room was awash with colour and the warmth of the flames radiated out into the house. Malic sat for a moment gazing into the fire, wishing that he could have shared this moment with Mila; but it was not to be. Instead, Malic stood up and took the drawing of Mila from the wall and walked over to his bed. He took the large cushion and the blanket from its frame and returned to the fireplace, where he laid them out and sat on them and as he looked into the flames, he held the drawing of Mila close to his chest. He gazed into the fire and watched as the sparks from the wood danced above the flames and disappeared up into the chimney. Although Malic was sad, the warmth of the fire and the portrait of Mila comforted him. He lay down in front of the fire, pulled the blanket over him and kissed the image of Mila. His eyes became heavy and before long, they slowly closed and Malic fell back into a deep sleep.

When the sun rose, the rays that shone in through the open back door woke Malic; he was still clutching the picture of Mila to his chest. He held it out and looked upon the image. Strangely, it made him smile. Malic then got up and placed the picture back on the nail on the wall above the fireplace. It had inspired him for the day of building that lay ahead. Malic crossed the room to the cupboard and took out some bread and cheese. His stomach rumbled with hunger. He took a slice of each, poured fresh water into his cup and ate. After he had finished eating, he sliced a little more of the bread and cheese and rolled it in some cloth. He took the, now empty, carafe of wine and filled it with cool water from the stream. Malic had learnt from the day before that if he was to get through that day, he would need to have plenty of water and food, to keep his energy up. Malic took his axe and left his house then headed for the clearing where he had chopped down the first tree he would use to build the temple.

All morning, Malic chopped and felled trees. He would build a frame for the roof of the temple out of wood, but the bottom would be made of stone. Around noon when the sun was high in the sky, Malic stopped working. His body ached and his hands where blistered from swinging his axe. Malic took out his food and the carafe of water and sat in the shade under a large tree. He unfolded the cloth and ate bread and cheese; washed down with the water from the stream. The bread and cheese filled his stomach, but his hands bled. After eating, Malic took the cloth that his food had been wrapped in and ripped it down the middle. He poured water on his wounds to clean them off and bound his hands in the cloth. Malic knew that he had to continue building the temple, as the spirit of the mountain had told him. He didn't know how it would help, but he was hoping that it would. Malic stood up and surveyed the area; there where rocks all around. He decided he would gather them into a pile in the middle where the temple would stand

and from there, he would build the foundations. Malic attempted to pick up one large rock that he thought would make a perfect small altar. His hands hurt when he tried to lift it; the rock weighed heavy on his small frame and the strength he used to have was no longer there. Lack of food and too much wine had taken its toll on Malic's, once strong, physique. Malic pushed the rock, trying to roll it into place at the centre of where the temple would stand, but it was too heavy. Not wanting to give up, he decided he would gather the smaller rocks from around the area and that's what he did. For hours, Malic lifted stones and piled them high; close to the centre of the clearing. The sun shone down hard and it drained Malic; his face was burnt and his hands were swollen. He could do no more and exhausted after a day's hard work, he made his way home.

When Malic arrived home, there was a large smoked leg of mutton wrapped in linen, leaning against his front door, with a note pinned to it. Malic picked up the note and read it, 'A gift.' Malic thought of Tobias and smiled to himself; the mutton was a welcome sight. He picked up the meat and entered the house. It was a relief for him not seeing the furniture strewn across the room, and he was glad he had taken the time to tidy his house the night before. Malic was hungry and decided he would make some food. He went into the kitchen and lifted the leg of mutton onto a hook he had placed in the wall for this very reason; then went to the cupboard. He opened it and looked inside. As well as the spices, vegetables and fruit there was a small pot of olive oil. Malic took the oil, the spices and the vegetables and placed them on the table. Even moving these small objects hurt his hands. He looked down at them; they were swollen and blistered. It was then that he remembered what Tobias had said to him about needing the ointment he left, for his hands. Malic went back to the cupboard and got the ointment; hoping that it would soothe and help his hands repair. He went outside to the stream, sat down and tried to undo the bindings he had put around his hands earlier. They had become stuck to the blisters that had formed there and when he tried to pull them off, the pain caused him to draw in a deep breath. Malic thought for a moment then knelt down at the water's edge. He reached out and held his hands in the cool water, which brought much needed relief from the pain that seared through them. After a short while, the water-soaked cloth had come unstuck and Malic peeled it from his hands. It was still painful but a lot less than before. He gently rubbed his hands together under the water and washed off the dry blood. The coolness of the water had made the swelling subside and his hands were now clean.

Malic stood up and went back into the house. He opened the ointment and the familiar smell, instantly took him back to his childhood. He remembered how his father had returned from a long stay on the mountain herding his flock. The long trek had made his father's feet swell and blister. He remembered how his mother sat his father down and washed his feet then dried them, and gently rubbed the same ointment into some cloth and bound them. The vivid memory of his precious mother brought tears to his eyes and Malic wiped them away with the back of his hand. "She's still teaching me now," he said out loud. He went back inside, took some clean cloth from the table and ripped it into two pieces then soaked it in the ointment. Taking each piece of material, he gently bound his hands. The ointment cooled them and the pain subsided.

After Malic had finished binding his hands he felt hungry. Again, thoughts of his mother entered his head. He remembered how, when his father was away on the mountain, he would help her cook. She would show him how to peel and slice the vegetables and which spices to add to the pot to make the food taste just perfect. No food he had ever tasted was like his mother's cooking. Malic needed to light the fire, so he cleared the hearth and filled it with the kindling from the barrel he had chopped the night before. There were two logs on the hearth and these would be enough to make a good fire. He took a match from the mantelpiece and lit the kindling. The small dry pieces of wood lit instantly and Malic placed the two logs carefully on top of them. The fire took and in no time at all, the flames lapped up the chimney. Malic took the small black pot from aside the fire and filled it with water from the stream. He placed it on the kitchen table next to the vegetables and then took his knife and peeled the vegetables: aubergines, peppers, onion and sweet potato. He chopped them to size and added them to the pot then took a pinch of each spice and stirred them into it. Malic took the pot and hung it on the hearth above the flames then returned to the cupboard and took out a plate and placed it on the table. He went over to the smoked mutton, cut through the linen and sliced two large pieces of meat from it and put them on the plate. He returned to cover the mutton leg but before he did, he couldn't resist slicing off a piece and popping it into his mouth. As he chewed the small piece of meat, the smoky flavour danced on his tongue and made his mouth water. It had been a long time since Malic had tasted anything so good. Malic went and sat by the fire. He gazed into the flames; occasionally stirring the stew, causing the sweet aroma of spiced vegetables to fill the room. As Malic stared into the flames, his mind wandered and he thought about how he would build the temple; how he would make it a monument to Mila and how it would be a testament of his love for her. For generations, people would gaze upon the great temple he had built and it would be a reflection of her beauty. The pot boiled over and sizzled on the hot embers of the fire, snapping Malic out of his daydream. He stood up, took a cloth and lifted the pot onto the kitchen table; the water had blended with the spiced vegetables and created a colourful, aromatic stew. Malic's mouth watered as he took a spoon and scooped some out onto the plate next to the slices of mutton. Steam rose from the plate into the air as he sat down and started to eat. It tasted delicious and Malic ate spoonful after spoonful of the tasty broth and smoked mutton. It was the first hot food he had eaten in weeks and it felt good to have such a familiar meal.

Malic cleared his plate then sat for a moment; his stomach was full and for the first time in a long time, he felt some kind of comfort. After a few minutes, Malic covered the pot with a linen cloth and went over to the fireplace. He picked up the cushion for the bed and the blanket, looked up at the drawing of Mila, kissed his fingers and reached out and placed them on the forehead of the portrait and wished her good night. Malic took the lavender oil Tobias had given him and just like he said, he poured a few drops of it onto the last burning embers of the fire. Instantly it evaporated and the sweet, musky smell of lavender filled the whole house. It reminded him of the smell of the valley in springtime and instantly gave him a sense of calmness. Malic went over to his bed and lay down and within seconds, he was asleep and that night, he dreamt of his beautiful Mila.

Daily, Malic would wake, make his food and fill his carafe with water, rub the ointment on his wounds, eat his fill, kiss the portrait of Mila goodbye and make his way to the mountain clearing to fell trees and gather stone. Every day when the sun was at its highest, he would stop to eat and drink his water; after which, he would sit under a tree in the warm shade and rest, always dreaming of Mila. Every time he awoke from his rest, the thought of Mila drove him on to build the temple in her honour. Each week on the same day, Malic would arrive home and there, wrapped in linen cloth left at his door, would be fruit, mutton, bread and cheese and Malic would say, 'Thank you' to Tobias, to himself, for leaving it there for him.

After a few of weeks and on a bright and sunny day, Malic arose early; as he always did now, feeling refreshed. Today was the day that he would start to erect the temple. He had worked hard but he knew that to build the temple, he would have to work even harder and longer. Malic prepared his food and made a little extra; as he knew today, would be a longer day than usual. He took two carafes of water and his food, kissed the portrait of Mila goodbye, took hold of his tool bag and headed out onto the mountain.

When Malic arrived at the mountain, he placed his food and carafes of water under the tree in the shade and turned to the large rock that he was unable to move a few weeks before. Malic approached the rock; he knew that this rock would be the flagstone for all the other rocks that would make his temple. He bent over and wrapped his arms around the rock and lifted, but the rock did not move. Malic tried with all his strength; his body shook and sweat poured from his brow, but still he could not move the rock. Malic tried and tried until eventually, he was forced by exhaustion, to give up. Tired and sweating, he went over and sat under the tree and picked up a carafe of water to drink. The sun was high in the sky and the midday heat was exhausting. The sun's rays burst through the branches of the tree, which gave little shade. Malic drank the cool water from the carafe and then raised it above his head and poured a little over it to cool himself down. He rubbed the water into his hair and across his face. As the water dripped down onto the sandy rock face,

Malic noticed a small beetle. The beetle was using a twig to move a ball of dung and started pushing it across the dusty ground. Malic watched fascinated at how the small beetle was able to move the dung, which was ten times its own size. He noticed that the beetle never stopped and it was the weight of the dung ball that carried itself; all it had to do was get it started and once the dung was rolling, the beetle just became the guide and steered it in the direction it wanted to go. Malic looked up at the rock and back down at the beetle and smiled, "Thank you little beetle, thank you," he said. As he did, he realised that those words of gratitude were the first words he had spoken aloud for quite some time and it made him feel good. Malic picked up his axe and went over to the rock. This time, instead of trying to lift it, he placed a smaller rock just in front of the bigger one and wedged his axe in-between the two. Malic pulled on the axe, causing the larger rock to lift and as it did so, he leant forward and pushed it. The rock rolled over and Malic jumped for joy. He danced around and whooped with delight. Just by being still, he had learned a valuable lesson from nature and the beetle. 'There are more ways than one when looking for a solution to a problem,' he thought, 'and sometimes we have to fail to find a way to succeed.'

Malic continued to work, moving the larger of the rocks into position first. The largest one would be the foundation, onto which he would then build the walls, using the smaller ones. Malic worked until it was dark and by the time he had finished, he had built the four small walls of the temple. Malic stood back and looked at what he had done. He experienced a feeling he had not had in a very long time; a sense of achievement and he felt proud. Malic lifted his axe and his carafe of water and made his way home.

Arriving home, Malic entered the house and went straight to the fireplace, where he kissed his fingers and touched them onto the lips of the drawing of Mila. Malic then gathered wood and kindling and lit the fire. He put the remainder of the broth he had made the night before, on the fire to warm through, and cut bread, which he then placed on the table. When the broth was hot, Malic poured it into his wooden bowl and ate it. The weeks of hard work on the temple had given him an appetite like never before. Malic was doing three things daily: eating, working and sleeping. Day after day he would work on the temple, come home and eat, kiss his beloved portrait of Mila and then sleep.

Twelve weeks of building, working, eating and sleeping had passed and the day had come when Malic knew that he would finish the temple.

He took his tools and made his way to the temple. Today he would lift the felled trees and hoist them onto the top of the walls that were now high enough for him to create the roof. Malic tied a rope to one end of the biggest tree and fed it over the edge of a small log he had wedged up high between the rock walls; which he'd built up over the weeks. Using the smaller log as a pulley system, he pulled the rope and lifted the tree trunk higher and higher. Malic pulled with all his strength; the weeks of working and eating had made him strong again. When the tree trunk was in position, Malic tied the rope to a rock on the ground and climbed up. He guided the large tree trunk into position so it sat along the centre of the temple; resting on the rock walls at either end. He then sat astride the large tree trunk and looked down onto the structure he had built. The walls were strong and high and he had built an archway in one wall, where he would put a wooden door. At the other end, he had left a small circular opening that the sun would shine through in the mornings.

Malic was happy with what he had achieved and wanted to get it finished. He was eager to return to the mountain and discover how he would use this temple to be with Mila once more. Maybe the spirit of the mountain had the power to bring her back. With that thought in his mind,

Malic continued to work on the roof of the temple. For three more days Malic worked on the roof, until it was finished. He then used the skills he had learnt from his father; whilst making the furniture for his house, to fashion a beautiful carved door, which he hung in the archway, completing the temple. Malic stood back and looked at what his hard work and dedication had achieved and for the first time in many months, he felt good about himself. Its walls were strong and its roof was watertight and secure. Above the large front door, he had fashioned from the finest wood, he had created a small bell tower. And today, he would go into the market and visit the farrier to ask him to make him a bell. Malic went home, put on his linen tunic, trousers and sandals and although he had no coins, he thought he might be able to find work at the market to pay for the bell. With this in mind, he set off to the market. Malic pulled the hood on his linen tunic up over his head to shade himself from the hot sun. He was tired and his body ached from the weeks of hard work he had done, but at the same time, he had found a new determination and was sure he would be able to find work.

As Malic approached the market he felt a strange surge run through him; a feeling of nervousness. It had been a long time since he had mixed with other people and it made his stomach churn, but he continued on. Everything around him sounded louder and looked brighter. The noise of the traders shouting out their sales pitches and the people who haggled their deals with them, sounded ten times louder than he remembered. Malic stood for a moment and drank in the colours of the spice-laden stalls that stood out against the pale sandy floor. The yellows, the reds and the oranges seemed to outshine the sun with their brilliance and the scent of fresh fruit filled the air. It stunned Malic; never before had he appreciated the sights, sounds and smells of the market in such a way. It was like a brand-new experience to him and it felt as though in all the years he had visited the market, this was the first time he really appreciated the beauty of it all.

Malic took a deep breath, closed his eyes and filled his lungs with the scents that surrounded him then turned and walked away; straight into the arms of Tobias. "Malic," Tobias said, "is that you?" Malic lifted his head, took his hood down and looked at Tobias,

"Yes Tobias, it is me; Malic." Tobias embraced Malic and held him tight.

"Malic, it is so good to see you. How are you? What have you been doing? I have thought about you so much, but I didn't want to disturb you in your time of grief." Malic pulled out of Tobias's kind embrace and looked at him.

"Well, if it hadn't been for you leaving me the food packages every week, I don't think I would be here right now and for that, I thank you." Tobias looked at him, slightly confused,

"But it was only one time, I felt I had to help somehow; it was the least I could do." Malic was confused,

"But you left me food each week; after I visited the mountain, it was at my door once a week when I arrived home from work. The cheese, the bread, the mutton…"

"I am sorry Malic, but it was not I who left you these things." Tobias held Malic by the shoulders and looked him up and down. "But come, come now and drink tea with me. What is important is that you are here now, yes?" Malic was still confused about who had been leaving him the food, but agreed and followed Tobias.

When they reached his stall, Tobias called for tea and food. They sat down at the back of the stall and a small boy brought through a tray of tea with spicy snacks and placed it on the fine rug that Tobias and Malic were sitting upon. Tobias poured two cups of tea and sprinkled mint into them, added a spoon of honey then passed one to Malic. Malic held the cup up to his lips and drank the warm tea; the sweetness of the honey danced across his tongue and the fresh taste of mint tingled in his throat. It had been a long time since Malic had drunk anything but fresh water and the tea tasted good. "So, Malic?" Tobias asked. "What have you been doing? Did you visit the mountain?" Malic was still trying to work out who it was that was leaving him the food, and came to the conclusion that it could only have been his father. Malic's quiet thoughts were broken by Tobias's question.

"I've been building a temple," Malic replied.

"A temple? Why a temple? What kind of temple?" asked Tobias.

"When I went to the mountain, the spirit of the mountain spoke to me. It told me that if I wanted to be with Mila again, I was to build myself a temple; so that is what I have done." Tobias sat quietly for a moment.

"Well, if this is what the spirit commanded, then building a temple was the right thing to do," Tobias said.

"I have," replied Malic, "it is finished. I came to market to get a bell from the farrier, but I have no coin; so I am seeking work to pay for it. I have good skills with wood and I can work hard," Malic explained. Tobias smiled then called out,

"Boy!" The young boy came running into the tent and stood in front of Tobias. Tobias whispered in his ear then the boy left as fast as he had arrived. Tobias took hold of Malic's hands; "I can see you have been working hard; the temple you have built must be a glorious sight to behold." Tobias let go of Malic's hand and changed the subject, "Malic, tell me, when was the last time you saw your father?" Malic had a feeling of shame come over him,

"I haven't seen my father in months," he said.

"He was here, I gave him one of my workers to help him with his herd and his harvest," Tobias told him. "I know that he has missed you, but he could not bear to see you as lost as you were." Malic looked shocked,

"You knew?" he stuttered, "about the wine?"

"There is not much that happens in this market that Tobias doesn't hear about, but sometimes a man has to be left to find out the error of his ways by himself." Malic sighed deeply and bowed his head,

"And of those errors, I am ashamed." Tobias held Malic by the arm,

"Malic, you have suffered a great loss and sometimes, when we experience loss, we retreat into our suffering; instead of sharing it. It is only when we go so far into the suffering we realise we have to get out, or be lost to it forever." Malic placed his hand on top of Tobias's,

"But inside, I still suffer. I have lost the person I have loved beyond all else. I don't understand how a temple will change all this, but building a temple is what the spirit of the mountain has asked me to do, so it is that I have done." Just then, the boy ran back into the tent, bringing with him a small package wrapped in cloth. Tobias took the package from the boy and handed it to Malic, who then unwrapped it to reveal a small golden bell. It shone bright in the few rays of sun that pierced the sides of Tobias's tent. "But how did you know?" Malic asked. Tobias smiled,

"Sometimes, it is better not to ask how or why, but just to be grateful for what is." Malic smiled and thanked Tobias, then wrapped the bell back up in the cloth. They both stood up and Malic embraced Tobias. Tobias pulled away, "Now go Malic. You have a temple to finish." Malic smiled at him,

"Thank you my brother." he said, then turned and started walking out of the tent.

"Malic!" Tobias shouted out, "If you want to know how building that temple will reunite you with Mila, I suggest you go back and ask the spirit of the mountain." Tobias smiled a knowing smile, "and one more thing," Tobias shouted, whilst still smiling; "take a look in that mirror." Malic was confused as he turned and left the tent. He walked through the stall and back into the market.

As he left, he saw Josiah sitting on the front of a cart laden with all kinds of grain, spices, cheese, bread and fruit and next to them, a pile of mutton wrapped in linen cloth. Malic instantly remembered the food that was left for him outside his door every week whilst he was building the temple. He thought Tobias, had been leaving it for him, but now he realised it wasn't; it was Jafkin's father, Josiah.

Malic stepped in front of Josiah's cart and it came to a halt. He walked around to the side where Josiah sat and Josiah looked down at him and then spoke softly,

"Malic, please climb up and sit with me." Malic, without thought and in silence, climbed onto the cart and sat next to Josiah. Josiah gently tapped the reins and the horses pulled the cart away out of the market.

Blame

Josiah and Malic sat in silence as the horses pulled the carriage out of the market and into the valley. The sun was hot and the trail was dusty. Pollen from the flowers in the valley hung heavy in the air and mosquitos buzzed around; causing the horses to swish their tails. After about an hour, when they neared Malic's house, Malic spoke, "Why did you leave me the food?" he asked. Josiah pulled on the reins and the horses came to a stop then Josiah calmly turned to Malic,

"It was all I could do," he said. "The last time I saw you was when I cut my son down from the tree outside your house and after that, there was never a suitable time for talking." Malic felt a surge of anger run through him; so he breathed in deep to calm himself. He looked at Josiah, wanting to shout all his anger into his face. He wanted to tell him of all the pain that he had suffered; the months of loneliness and turmoil he had been through. How he would never get to marry the woman he loved because of Josiah's jealous, selfish son. He wanted to scream out all the heartache and suffering he had endured and for Josiah to feel the same pain he had felt since losing Mila, but instead, as he looked further into Josiah's eyes, all he could see were empty, soulless, tear-filled pools. The life that once filled Josiah eyes, had gone; replaced with a bleak and empty blackness. Malic stared at Josiah for a moment and he saw the pain and suffering he had endured, etched into his face. Where there once sat a proud, strong man now sat a frail, worn-out shell of an empty soul. It was obvious that Josiah had already experienced the same pain and anguish that he had and there was nothing that Malic could say or do to make Josiah suffer more. Josiah's eyes filled with tears as Malic sat and stared at him. "Forgive me," he whispered; his voice trembled and tears fell from his eyes as he spoke. Malic felt all the anger inside him diminish and it was replaced with a feeling of pity. Malic knew that Josiah had no price to pay him for his actions; that debt was already being paid. Malic thought back to the conversation with his father about revenge and the words he had said to him that night in his house,

'My boy, do you not understand? If you seek revenge, then you become just like him.'

Malic looked at Josiah as he sat there weeping like a child. Sadness ran out of every pore of his skin; the pain of heartbreak flooded out of him with every tear. It saddened Malic to see Josiah like this; he reached out and embraced Josiah and held him tight. As he comforted him, he knew that although Jafkin had only suffered death once, Josiah was reliving it every second of every day. Malic spoke, "Josiah, I am sorry for your loss. I am sorry that, you too had to suffer as I have. I am sorry that we both lost someone we love. I understand Josiah that you are not your son, I understand that you tried to give your son the best you could; what father wouldn't? I am sorry Josiah that Jafkin never understood, as you do, that love cannot be taken; love only exists when it is freely given." Malic pulled away from his embrace and wiped the tears from Josiah face, "Josiah, Jafkin took away my true love, but for that, you are not at fault and forgiveness is not needed from me. I see the pain and suffering you have lived through, just as I have and no innocent man deserves to suffer for something that was out of his hands. Please Josiah, live your life with peace in your heart; you owe me no debt and no favour. I hope the spirit of the mountain speaks to you; like it has to me and your pain and suffering is lifted." With that, Malic picked up the cloth bundle that contained the temple bell and climbed down from the cart and as he started to walk away, Josiah spoke to him,

"I have been to the mountain and the spirit of the mountain has spoken to me." Malic stood still as Josiah continued, "The spirit told me to feed and comfort the lost people of the world and that would bring me peace and lead me to my true calling." Josiah's eyes changed and a new light shone in them. "And now, because of your words, I know what I must do; I now know my true calling."

"And what is that?" asked Malic.

"I will open the doors of my home to the poor and those that suffer. I will provide work and food for those that have none, I will create a refuge in the market where people will come and know what it is to be loved." Malic smiled and felt at peace. He bowed his head at Josiah, turned and made his way back to his home.

When Malic arrived home, he looked for the small mirror the trader had left for him many weeks ago. He thought about the last words Tobias had said to him; telling him to look in the mirror. Malic picked it up, turned it towards himself and looked into it. Looking back at him, Malic hardly recognised the face he saw. His beard was long and the skin around his eyes had wrinkled. The sun had tanned his skin and etched lines ran, like dried-out streams, across his forehead. Malic's hair was long, covered in dust and matted in parts. The once boyish face of Malic had gone and now, staring back at him was the face of a man; who knew what it was like to have loved and to have lost. Malic looked up from the mirror and over at the drawing of Mila that hung on the nail above the hearth. He then looked back at his reflection. He realised he had let himself and Mila down and had lost all respect for himself. Malic remembered how, before he would go and see Mila, he would shave and take a bath; he would always make sure that he was looking his finest. Tomorrow, he thought to himself, 'I will go and hang the bell in the tower, and tomorrow I will speak to the spirit of the mountain and the spirit will reunite me with my Mila. If I am to see her again, I must be at my best.' Malic placed the mirror on the table then went outside and gathered wood and lit the fire. He filled the large pot and a few smaller ones with water from the stream and hung them over the fire. He took off his dust-ridden linen trousers and tunic; knelt down at the stream and washed them in the water then hung them up on a small tree to dry. As he went back inside he took the, now boiling, water that was in the pots and filled the small wooden bath that sat in the room at the back of the house. He filled the bath with the hot water then went back into the house, opened the cupboard and took out the lavender oil. He returned with it to the bath and poured some of the oil into the warm water. The aroma of fresh lavender filled the room. Malic picked up a bucket and filled it with cold water from the stream outside, took it inside and poured it into the bath. Steam billowed and filled the room. Malic stepped into the bath; the water was warm and welcoming. He put both feet over the side and lay down in the water. As he stretched out his legs, he instantly felt the water and oil sooth his skin. Malic reached over the side and picked up the soap. He wet his hair and rubbed it with the soap. A thick lather formed as he scrubbed and washed it causing the soapsuds to run black. Malic had always washed his face and hands but he hadn't bathed in weeks and the colour of the water reflected that. He finished washing his hair then leant forward and dipped his head under the warm, now soapy, water. He rubbed his hands through his hair; it was long and black and it stuck to his face and neck. He scooped it back with his hands and squeezed away the excess water, leaving it to fall down the centre of his back. Malic took the soap and stood up. He washed his body and then sat back down and rinsed it off. He laid back and relaxed for a while before stepping out of the wooden tub and when he looked back into it, the water was almost black with dirt and a thin layer of grey suds had formed on top. Malic couldn't understand how he had let himself become so unkempt, but was glad that now, he was clean and felt fresh. He picked up the lavender oil and the soap, went back into the house and placed them next to the hearth. He then went over to the bed and looked under it. There were the blankets that Mila's mother and the women of the village had made. He took one of them and wrapped it around himself to dry off. He pulled out another and took it, along with the cushion from the bed and laid it down in front of the fire. Placing the blanket over the top of it, he then went to the cupboard and took out some cheese, some bread and carved some mutton with his knife. He poured some water from his carafe into a cup and took it, along with his food, the knife and the mirror from the table and placed it all on the floor in front of the fire. Malic sat down on the cushion and ate the food and drank the cool fresh water. Once he had eaten his fill, he placed the empty plate of food to one side and picked up the mirror. He looked into it and although his skin was weathered, his eyes and hair looked brighter; but his beard was long. Malic picked up the soap and dipped it in the pot of water that hung next to the fire. He lathered it up and rubbed it into his beard. Malic then took his knife and tested it for sharpness, by rubbing his thumb over the edge of it from side to side. The thin edge of the blade sprung slightly; it was sharp. Malic placed the mirror on the hearth and began to shave. He dragged the edge of the blade down his cheek, scraping off the thick hair that had grown into a long beard. The soap helped the blade glide and kept Malic's skin supple. He took his time and after a while, he had shaved his beard off. He leant over the pot of water and rinsed his face then took a corner of the blanket he was wrapped in and dried it. Malic picked up the mirror and stared into it. This time, although weathered and looking slightly worn, Malic recognised the man looking back. His skin was dark and his eyes shone white; in fact, he didn't think he had ever seen his eyes glow so bright. Malic put the mirror down and took the portrait of Mila from the wall. He sat down by the fire and admired the beautiful image of her face. Then he picked up a piece of kindling and his knife and placed the drawing on the blanket next to him and the kindling beside it. The kindling was a little longer than the drawing, so Malic picked it up and cut it to the same size. He picked up three more pieces and started to fashion them into a frame. After a few minutes of cutting and scraping, Malic had created a wooden frame for the picture of Mila. He stood up and held it out in front of him then hung it on the nail on the wall. He sat back down, arranged the blanket on the cushion then lay down with his eyes fixed on the image of Mila. He felt a stirring inside him and wondered if the spirit of the mountain would soon reunite him with her. Malic lay there in front of the fire as the soft orange and red glow of the flames filled the room. He was warm and comfortable and after a while, his eyes became heavy and the last thing he saw before he fell asleep was the face of his beloved Mila.

The spirit returns

Malic woke the next morning, stood up, stretched his arms out wide and stood high on his toes. His whole body creaked and cracked; the weeks of hard work he had endured had made his bones tight and his muscles stiff. He tilted his head from one side to the other; stretching out his neck, and then relaxed. He felt good after stretching out his tired muscles. Malic walked through the house to the back door and opened it. The sun shone through and the air was warm. The sound of the flowing stream filled his ears and birds sang in the trees. He went over to the tree where he had hung his linen trousers and top and got dressed. He knelt down next to the stream and cupped the cool fresh water in his hands and splashed it on his face. It wasn't until then that he remembered; he had shaved his beard off. His skin felt rough to the touch but not having the beard, made him feel cleaner and he felt better for shaving it. Malic wet his hair and ran his fingers through it; letting it fall behind his head. It had grown more than he thought in such a short time, but he liked it and would keep it that way. Malic went back into the house and there on the table, sat the golden bell. Today, he would take the bell and hang it in the tower; completing the temple the spirit had told him to build. Malic was nervous and full of anticipation. He wondered how the spirit of the mountain would reunite him with Mila.

He slipped on his sandals then took the portrait of Mila from above the fireplace and some rope from the cupboard, wrapped the bell, the rope and the picture in some cloth and made his way out of the house. Malic set off through the valley and up the mountain to the temple. When he reached the clearing, he unwrapped the golden bell, picked it up along with the rope, and climbed up the side of the temple to the top of the small tower. Malic threaded the rope through the top of the bell and fastened it tight inside the tower and then climbed back down. He stood back and looked at what he had built. He was proud of the small temple that stood there on the side of the mountain in honour of his love that was lost. Malic picked up the picture of Mila and walked into the temple. Inside it was cool, but the round opening he had left at the back of the small room let the sun shine through onto a large rock he had built into the wall opposite. Malic knelt down and placed the picture of Mila on the rock. He stared at the picture then waited. He didn't know what he was waiting for, but he had completed the task the spirit of the mountain had set him so now he waited expectantly. He knelt there for what seemed like hours. The air was still and the sun had moved around and was no longer shining through the opening in the wall. Malic was becoming frustrated; his knees hurt from kneeling for so long on the rough stony floor and his back and neck had become stiff. Just as Malic was about to stand, he felt a cold shadow fall across his face. His skin prickled and a cold shiver ran right through his body. He kept his eyes closed as fear gripped him and his body froze. The air became colder still and then, on the back of his neck he felt a hot breath, then a low growl that became louder, the longer it went on. It was the black wolf. Malic thought that the spirit of the mountain had tricked him and for him and Mila to be together again today, the black wolf would take his life. He shook with fear and waited for the sharp teeth of the wolf to pierce his skin and rip away at his flesh, ending his life. Just as he expected the black wolf to strike and take his life, a warm wind blew through the opening in the wall and the golden bell above his head rang out. Malic opened his eyes and there, in front of him was Mila's face. Malic seized his chance. He spun around fast with his fist clenched, to strike the black wolf hard across its face. But as he swung around, he hit out into emptiness, causing him to fall onto floor. The temple room was empty. Malic turned around expecting to see Mila; but all he saw was the picture he had placed upon the shelf. Malic was confused. He got to his feet and looked around the room. It was cold and still. Anger struck Malic in the pit of his stomach, which then radiated out of every pore of his skin. He ran out of the temple and looked up into the sky; the rage flowed through him as he screamed as loud as he could. "WHY? WHY WOULD YOU PUT ME THROUGH THIS? WHY HAVE YOU TORTURED ME SO?" Malic spun around on the spot looking towards the sky and in his anger, tore off his linen tunic and threw it to the ground. Tears of anger flowed from his eyes as he fell to his knees clenching his fists and slamming them into the ground. Again he shouted out; this time, towards the ground, "WHY HAVE YOU BROKEN MY HEART AND RIPPED MY SOUL APART? WHY? WHY? Malic cradled his head in his hands and sobbed. It was then he heard a voice boom out inside his head,

"My son, stand up and listen to me." Malic had heard this voice before; it was the spirit of the mountain.

"Why should I listen to you, look what you have done. You have taken everything I have ever loved away from me and set me a fruitless quest to build this damned temple." Malic turned and pointed to the temple he had built. The voice spoke out again; except this time it was calmer and more peaceful.

"Malic, my beautiful son; listen to me. When you came to me at this mountain, the black wolf challenged you. Many times through history, the black wolf has challenged countless men on this mountain. Some pass, but many have failed." Malic was confused,

"What challenge?" he asked. The spirit spoke again,

"Fear, Malic. The challenge of fear. You came to ask me how you would live your life without the woman you loved. But before I could tell you, I had to know you were ready to face your greatest fears. The wolf, the black wolf, is just that; a manifestation of your greatest fears." The spirit continued, "Many men who gave in to their fears on this mountain, lost their lives to the black wolf and I had to know you were ready for what was to come." Malic realised that the black wolf had never truly lived, except in the hearts and minds of men; men who had become so scared to live, they had given their lives for an unfounded fear. Malic stood firm; his mind had calmed, but he was confused,

"But this temple, why did you tell me to build this temple if it was a pointless task?" The spirit spoke softly,

"Malic, my son, when you came to me, I told you to build *yourself* a temple; in honour of your love for Mila. I told you to build it strong and on a solid foundation; and that you have done. But Malic, this temple of wood and stone is not the temple you honour the memory of your love with. Malic, it is *YOU, YOURSELF, YOU ARE THE TEMPLE!"* Malic was shocked. He didn't understand.

"What do you mean?" Malic called out.

"Malic, look at yourself. By cutting these trees down, you made your arms strong. By moving this stone, your legs have grown in strength. Whilst building this temple of stone, you have eaten well and you no longer sit in sadness drowning in wine; pining for her. You have slept well and looked upon the picture of your love that has passed and it has filled your heart with joy, instead of sadness and heartbreak. Malic, YOU are the temple and the life you live now is how you will honour your love for Mila." Malic stood for a moment and looked at himself. His torso was strong and his arms and legs rippled with muscles developed from the hard work building the temple and from the good food he had been eating. Malic realised that the days spent working had taken his mind away from the heartache and pain and helped him concentrate on the moment he lived in. Walking through the valley and climbing the mountain every day had given him purpose to live again. Malic spoke out softly,

"But what about Mila?" he asked.

"Malic, I told you when you came to the mountain that life is life and death is death and not even I, the spirit of this mountain can change that. But Malic, the hope you had in your heart kept you strong and kept you going. When you were confronted by the wolf inside the temple and you faced a certain death, you could have given up, but the bell rang and the vision of Mila standing there waiting for you, made you strong and you killed that fear and in turn, the black wolf, and now you can live again." Calmness came over Malic; calmness he had not felt since he sat under the stars in the valley and declared his love for Mila and gave her the necklace. The spirit spoke again,

"Malic, look out into the valley. Do you see the beauty of the flowers and the nature that resides there? Do you see the birds in the blue sky? Do you see the trees that stand tall and the stream that flows through it; breathing life into the valley?" Malic looked out across the valley. The sun was setting and shone onto the mountain in the distance, lighting it up in all its glory. Malic had never seen a more beautiful sight. The spirit continued, "Malic, your spirit comes from the mountain and from the valley and when your life here in this world is over, your spirit returns home. Malic, Mila lives on. She lives in the flowers and the trees; she lives in the water that flows through the valley. She lives in the mountain that protects it; she lives in the sun and the stars. She lives in the moon that lights up the valley at night and Malic, she lives on the wind." At that moment, a warm wind blew through the valley and the sound of the bell at the top of the tower rang out. Malic turned and looked at the bell. He realised that it was Mila who had saved him from his own fears, it was Mila who had saved him from the black wolf and it was Mila that wanted him to live. Malic's heart filled with love and his empty soul felt full once more as the warm wind blew. He could smell Mila's sweet perfume and as the bell rang out, he could hear her voice. Tears of happiness fell from Malic's eyes as the spirit spoke to him for the final time, "Malic, do not live in the past or feel sad that you are without Mila, for she is always with you. She looks down on you, on everything you do. And when she does, it is not the tears of a sad, lonely, broken man she wants to see. It is the man that stands here now; strong in honour of the love that surrounds him. Remember Malic, you are the temple; built in honour of the love you have for Mila." Silence fell and all that could be heard was the sound of the golden bell, gently ringing out across the valley. It was at that moment, Malic knew the spirit had left. Malic sat on the edge of the cliff and as a gentle breeze blew, the bell continued to ring out softly and Malic knew that Mila was with him

Epilogue

Malic sat listening to the soft sound of the bell ringing in the breeze; he smiled to himself as he looked out onto the valley. He could see the spot where he sat and asked Mila to be his wife. That thought, that not so long ago had crippled him with sadness, now warmed his heart. As he looked at that spot, he saw two men walking towards him. It was Malic's father with the young man, Emile who worked his fields. Malic smiled and looked up at the golden bell hanging above the stone temple and smiled, "Thank you," he said. Then he got up and made his way down into the valley to meet his father. His father saw him approaching and stopped as Malic continued walking towards him. As Malic stopped in front of him, his father smiled and his eyes filled with tears of joy. Malic stepped forward and embraced him. He held him tight, feeling the comfort of his father's arms; that he had missed so much. His father kissed Malic's cheeks then stood back and as he did, they heard a horse and cart coming down the path beside them. The cart was stacked high and was laden with pots and pans, spices and food, bottles and jugs, fine clothes and woven tapestries. Malic couldn't make out who was on the cart at first but as it drew closer, he saw that it was Tobias. "Malic," Tobias shouted out in his usual jovial voice, "I see you have been to the mountain."

"Yes," Malic replied.

"And your temple?" Tobias asked. Malic looked down at himself then at his father,

"My temple is built."

Tobias laughed,

"Here," he shouted, "your father dropped it at my stall." Tobias threw a small bag to Malic; which he caught. Just then, Emile shook Malic's father's hand and bowed his head then ran and jumped onto the moving cart. Malic looked down into his hand and opened the bag. He pulled out what was inside; it was the necklace with the emerald green stone. Malic's father then spoke,

"I took it from around her neck before she returned to the mountain. I thought you would like to keep it, to remember her." Malic smiled at his father and held the necklace tight in his hand.

"I will remember her Father, with everything I say and everything I do, because she is with me everywhere I go."

Tobias's cart passed them by, churning up a swirl of dust as it made its way along the path towards the setting sun and the sound of the golden bell rang out across the valley...

The End

CPSIA information can be obtained
at www.ICGtesting.com
Printed in the USA
LVOW08s0332021116
511207LV00018B/1946/P